carry you

carry you

GLORI SIMMONS

Autumn House Press

PITTSBURGH

Autumn House Press receives state arts funding support through a grant from the Pennsylvania Council on the Art, a state agency funded by the Commonwealth of Pennsylvania, and the National Endowment for the Arts, a federal agency.

ISBN: 978-1-938769-29-0
Library of Congress Control Number: 2017960548

Cover art: "Hand of Fatima II" courtesy of Ayad Alkadhi. www.aalkadhi.com

contents

I

II

III

for Michael and Olive

Who among us belongs to another:
Do you, with the wrinkled face?
Or we, guardians of the road to no return?
Or do we all, Baghdad,
belong to the executioner?

—Fawzi Karim, "The Scent of Berries"

I

FEMALE DRIVER

SAHAR KHALIL shook the metal gate in front of her home. She was overheated and out of breath. The gate's remote control was clipped to the sun visor in her car blocks away. She'd just walked the distance in the late afternoon sun in a pair of new shoes she'd purchased based solely on the shape of the heel. Her sunglasses slid down her nose. Her skirt and blouse stuck to her skin in unflattering places. Her shoulder ached from the weight of her purse. She took hold of a crossbar on the gate and the hot metal burned her palms. She ignored the pain, letting her shoes drop off as she climbed.

After a few long, painful steps, she straddled the top. On one side was the row of white-and-pink stone houses with ornate verandas suggesting classical and colonial pasts. In the other direction, more homes and shops, men returning from work carrying briefcases. She could no longer see the gas station, which must have re-opened for business by now. From here, it looked as if nothing had happened. Still, there was the bitter aftertaste of vomit in her throat, the bump on her forehead, the need to get away. She placed both hands on the top of the gate and twisted her body so she could ease herself down on the other side. Not so much an ease, as it turned out, but a sudden drop, her body flapping against the gate like a rug being beaten clean. Her sunglasses hit the ground. A lens popped out. She held on tightly as she felt around with her foot for the closest crossbar. When she reached the ground, the urge to run was still there, but now there was also the temptation to curl into a ball and moan. On the other side of the gate, her new shoes stood without her—as if she'd evaporated into thin air.

Sahar adjusted her purse and skirt, and limped, sweaty and dehydrated, toward the house. The neighbor's maid looked up from watering a lemon tree on her veranda, but politely pretended not to notice her. Sahar pushed open the door to her house and stepped into the dim entry, shedding her support hose, dirty and shredded on the bottoms of her feet. As the air hit her blistered toes, it felt as if she were being stung by bees.

Her family swarmed. "Are you OK? What happened to you? *Tsk, tsk.* Here, let me help you. Mum." It hurt her eyes to see them. So lovely, so innocent and alive, so whole. Sahar's husband, Qaseem, grabbed her under the arms and led her to the sofa. Nalah, her mother-in-law, took a quick inventory of the situation and left the room. Realizing her hands were smeared with blood, Sahar closed them into fists. Her son Jamal frowned. As always, his fear registered as doubt. Leila, his twin, watched from behind her brother with tears running down her cheeks. Sahar wanted nothing more than to take her two children into her arms and plead for their forgiveness. Instead, she smiled and collapsed onto the couch.

Nalah returned with a small copper tray and a glass of sweetened tea, which she handed to Sahar without a word. A sure sign of her disapproval. Sahar took the cup in her trembling hands and blew through the steam. When she set the cup back down, the blood from her hands left a pink smear along the edge. Qaseem gently lifted Sahar's feet over the armrest so that he could examine the blistered tops of her toes. Shaking his head at the open sores, Qaseem finally said, "Leila and Jamal, fetch warm water and a cloth. Bandages too."

Their daughter ran, always happy to be of help. Jamal, more interested in being with the adults, stalled until his grandmother shooed him away. Neither had ever seen their mother injured. Qaseem carefully placed a pillow under Sahar's calves and another under her neck as Nalah looked on. He glanced in the direction of the children and then whispered, "What happened? Was it a car accident? Should I call a doctor, my love?"

All Sahar could say was no, locking eyes with him. Not now, she thought. Not in front of *her*. Qaseem, more concerned than before, nodded as the children returned to the room. He sat on the edge of the couch and held her bloody hand. Jamal lugged in a pot of water that sloshed over the edges as he set it at the end of the couch. Leila followed with a washcloth and the box of bandages. Without being asked, she dipped the cloth into the water and wrung it out. "Tell me if this hurts, Mum," she said as she wiped the dirt off the soles of Sahar's feet. When Qaseem attempted to take the rag from Leila, Sahar stopped him.

Each of Leila's caresses seemed to erase a piece of the day. Smiling, Sahar tried to remember when she'd been pampered like this in the past. Was it the morning she'd begun to bleed, waking from lurid dreams to find her bedding stained? It had been an overcast day in London and was the only school day that her mother ever let her skip. For hours she lay in bed with the hot water bottle pressed to her belly. Later, she and her mother drizzled honey and pistachios onto dough as Sahar became accustomed to the new awareness of her body's internal workings. It felt as if someone was tugging a string inside of her and everything would gush out if she moved the wrong way. Or had it been following the birth of the twins as the doctors made sure there would be no infection in the incision below her abdomen? She'd been in a room that overlooked the Tigris, in a hazy shock. In either case, there existed the fact that life would never be the same again.

She looked back down at her daughter who had the precise, unapologetic touch of a surgeon. The washing of feet was part of the wedding ritual to prepare the bride. Raised in London, Sahar found most tradition smothering, but had enjoyed the circling of women at the henna party. With her gaze on her daughter, Sahar paraphrased as best she could remember, a poem Qaseem had once recited in their early days, "This is love: to cause a hundred veils to fall, to take a step without feet."

Leila opened Sahar's bloody hands to wash them as well. "Mum, tell us what happened."

"Oh, darling, it was terrible," Sahar lied. "A dog ran in front of the car and I couldn't stop in time."

For weeks afterward, Leila would ask about the dog: What color was it? What kind? Was it a puppy or old? Did it whimper? Did it limp? Where did it bleed? Did it die? In the story that Sahar told her daughter, she'd carried the bleeding dog to the side of the road where it got back to his feet and then stood dazed for a moment before running off. At times, that was how Sahar remembered that afternoon as well. She'd hit a stray dog that had wandered into the street. The dog had survived.

Sahar had always loved to drive. It was physical. When she slid into the leather driver's seat, her shoulders dropped a good inch, her breathing deepened. It wasn't erotic like the car advertisements in England had suggested, but calming, a pleasure that was hers and hers alone.

That morning, not wanting to ruin the heels on her new pumps, she removed them and set the pair in the passenger seat next to the lunch Nalah had prepared for her. She searched her purse for her favorite Estée Lauder lotion, something she'd worn since she was a teenager admiring the sophisticated cosmetics girls at Fenwick on Bond Street. With the recent sanctions, she now had to ask her friends to send it to her via airmail. She rubbed it into her knuckles and temples, breathing in what she'd once identified as the scent of midnight and now simply associated with her youth. Passing through the white gate, she felt nothing short of jubilant.

She shook a cigarette loose from the pack she kept hidden in her glove compartment and slipped it between her lips. She pushed in the lighter and then a Best of Streisand cassette, adjusting the levels so that the American's strange nasal voice came through the back speakers. She cracked open the top of the window and blew out her first puff of smoke. Every move was steeped in ritual. On the boulevard, she sang with Babs, sometimes even cried. She was a teenager in London again, her future still mysterious. She'd become exactly what she'd hoped for back then, a woman who had it all: a husband, career, children, a car, and for several months now, a lover. In her car, she could appreciate the fact with satisfaction. She didn't know another woman with so much.

Sahar's need for independence was something her mother-in-law refused to understand. Every morning as Nalah handed Sahar a bag of lunch, she used the same skeptical tone: "I'm not sure what a working woman eats. I hope it is good enough." Every day when Sahar arrived at the museum she inspected the contents of the bag— foil-wrapped rice and tomato salad—and then dropped it into the garbage can just outside the lobby. She was a busy woman. Most days, she went without lunch. Every afternoon when she got home, she assured Nalah that it had been delicious.

That morning, before leaving the house, Sahar overheard Nalah tell Jamal to come so she could help with her little prince's shoes the way she'd done for her sons. *Prince*, the word exasperated Sahar. The shoes in question did not even have laces. From where Sahar stood, she could see down the hall to Leila, already dressed, pouring imaginary tea into her doll's pursed lips. She rested the teacup on the upper lip and tipped down, such a sweet, innocent error. She hoped Leila hadn't heard the nonsense coming from her grandmother. From Sahar's point of view, there were already too many princes in the world. She wanted both of her children to have everything. Sahar smiled, remembering Jamal's response.

"Sons?" he'd asked his grandmother, suddenly curious. "But you have only father."

That had quieted down Nalah. Sahar barely knew her brother-in-law, Youssef, a ruffian, angry and undone from his service in the war against Iran. Most conversations with him had ended with her holding a pamphlet that interpreted the scripture passionately. Were they about hijab or Western invasion? She didn't remember now. But the general sense she had was that he was criticizing her. He left the country years ago, and no one had heard from him since.

"Where is your spoiled prince now?" Sahar asked into the car in English, as the speedometer hit 130 kph. "Is he even wearing shoes?"

Sahar turned onto the Adhamiyah Bridge, passing over the Tigris to the west side. She admired the early morning sunlight ricocheting off the metal cables that swooped down from the center of the bridge like graceful arms. She loved not knowing how or why the bridge stood, but that it simply did—the fact that each day she was asked to trust in something larger than herself and she could. It was as close to faith as she'd ever get. An oncoming tank nosed its way into her lane. She honked and swerved. It was undoubtedly headed to Kuwait where Saddam was once again attempting to take what wasn't his. Another example of princedom.

On this side of the tinted windows, Sahar felt as if she could finally be who she was. She could smoke a cigarette. She could sing the songs of an American Jew. She could curse the Iraqi Army. Question the president. Speak the Queen's English. Talk back to her mother-in-law. Even ridicule her missing brother-in-law.

Out the car window, the city's pale skyline came into view. A blue minaret intersected the horizon line. She passed the stadium and then the cemetery. She put out her cigarette. At the red light, she twisted her rearview mirror down, slipped her sunglasses to the tip of her nose, and applied her eyeliner. It took a steady hand to trace the eyelid without a quiver, even as her bare foot lifted softly from the brake and the car eased toward the intersection. It was the same kind of steadiness required to reapply gold leaf, lift an ancient sherd with a pair of tweezers, or write a series of tiny accession numbers on the underside of a jar. She had a meeting with the museum director and head of collections in an hour. Unfortunately, with the possibility of an American invasion, her first task as chief conservator was to help "hide the silver" as she'd once heard a British curator say about his work during the World War. Today they would devise a plan—prioritize the past and start tucking it safely away.

After the seemingly endless meeting, Sahar crossed the Sinak Bridge to meet her lover, an archeology professor who brought his students into the museum once a semester for a private tour. His apartment sat above an antique shop on the edge of the Old City. He'd rented it for another lover. This fact amused Sahar, even comforted her in a perverse way. She was replaceable; she could leave any time.

Sahar parked around the corner. Before getting out of the car, she took a scarf from her glove box and wrapped it closely under her chin and then slid on her sunglasses. The meeting at work had made her late by an hour, but she knew he often remained in his apartment to do research in the afternoons, sitting at the small desk that faced the window overlooking the street. She reached into her purse for the key as she climbed the narrow stairs. By the time she'd arrived at the apartment door, she'd shed her disguise. Some days they made love hastily between their appointments. Other days they lingered, discussing art or archeology in their underwear, drinking Turkish coffee.

When she opened the door, there he sat in his plush chair, his reading glasses perched on the tip of his nose, his legs crossed, a book open on his knee. He looked up, smiling at her, his finger lingering on the line he'd just read. He folded the corner of the page. This small act made the conservator in her cringe, the adulterer in her aroused. He closed the book and set it down on the floor. She slipped off her new shoes and reached up under her linen skirt to pull down her hose and underwear, stepping out of them on her way to him. How easy it was: her body encompassing his with little maneuvering. No small detail or argument to hold them back. No children sleeping on the other side of the walls. No mother-in-law getting up to go pee.

"What are you reading?" she asked as she slowly lifted and lowered herself.

"A history of Asmar. I may take a group of students there in the summer."

"A dig?" she said with a sigh, closing her eyes. She was thinking of the memo from the minister of culture, which more or less confirmed an American attack. She doubted there would be a dig. Sahar concentrated on the sensations under her skirt, the way her body felt simultaneously swollen and starved. He freed her blouse from her skirt waistband and slid his hands up her belly and over her bra. On the small table behind the couch, a jar glowed in the sunlight. "Is that honey?" she asked.

"From the family almond farm."

As they had sex, Sahar pictured him in the mornings, the newspaper on the table, a hard roll on a plate, the honey. He would be thinking of them: his wife and the four boys. Somehow, even with everything Sahar had, he had more.

On the way home that afternoon, the line at the gas station was several cars deep. The two brothers who worked at the station ran back and forth trying to keep the line moving. Next door, a woman watched over a group of children as they played in the shade of a palm tree close to the exit. In general, Sahar was not fond of other people's children, but these sometimes waved when she left the station. She counted them. Nine. The little girls covered head-to-toe in black, their long skirts dust-rimmed. From a distance, they looked like tiny women. The boys, in shorts, ran about kicking a soccer ball.

Sahar wasn't the only privileged woman who stopped here for petrol, yet the elder brother became unpleasant when taking orders from a bareheaded woman behind the wheel. The younger could be kind, offering to wash her windows or check the oil without accepting a tip. Trying to calculate which brother she would have, Sahar reached for the scarf she kept in her purse for visiting her lover and sacred sites for her job. Contradictions were a part of life in Iraq, more so for a woman who was registered as a Ba'ath Party member and chief conservator of a national museum, yet did not support the president. When the nice brother walked up to her window, she let the scarf drop to the seat.

She watched him in her rearview mirror as he filled the tank. He walked to the front of her car with a rag to wash her windows. Dirty water dripped down the sides. She found something pleasing in his gray eyes, his sun-worn skin, his fingernails black with oil. Her stomach growled. Sahar tried to remember what lunch had been, so she could thank Nalah, and remembered the honey she'd slipped into her purse when the archeologist had gone into the bathroom. She took the jar out and pushed the wax seal down with her finger. It was light, a spring batch. She stuck her finger in deeper and then brought it to her tongue, letting the honey dissolve in her mouth.

Feeling watched, Sahar's eyes met the attendant's through the windshield. She licked her finger again and then pushed the wax back into place, smiling at him as she wiped her sticky finger on the scarf. When he returned to her side window, she placed the payment into his hand plus a little extra, and then rolled up the window before he could say no.

She started up the car and pushed in her lighter. It would be a two-cigarette day. Someone behind her honked. As she eased the car past the pumps, something white flew in front of her. Out of the corner of her eye, she saw one of the children, a boy, running toward the ball. She slammed on the brakes, cranking the steering wheel as if there were still time. A thud—unmistakably, irrevocable—came from her fender. The child flew up onto her windshield. Both of their heads slammed into the glass at the same time, his frightened eyes catching hers as the car skidded to a stop.

What had just felt like a slow arabesque sped up. Sahar jumped out of the car and ran to the boy who was sprawled on the ground. His eyes were open, blood gushed from his nose. She knelt down and placed his head on her lap, wiping the blood from his nose with her scarf. The rise and fall of his chest were nearly imperceptible. A woman screamed from across the street and ran toward them, pushing away the crowd. "Rasheed, my little prince," the woman cried as she sank to the ground, yanking the scarf from Sahar's hand and pushing her away. "Don't touch him, you beast." Too shaken to drive, Sahar walked home.

On the drive to and from work, there was no way to avoid the area. Passing by, she steadied her gaze on the road as if watching for dogs that might run into her path. As an act of contrition, she stopped seeing the professor without even a word. A few months later an American bomb obliterated the area and presumably the families along with it. The next time it was safe for Sahar to drive to work, all she could locate of the station was the charred trunk of a palm tree. Intertwined with the shame and sorrow was a thread— golden and strong—of relief. Her mistake had been erased. She turned up the music.

She crossed the Sinak Bridge and returned to the narrow street with the antique store for the first time since the accident. She parked across the street and got out of the car without covering her head. The store windows had been boarded up, but the door was wide open. The owner rested in an old chair, sipping coffee from a demitasse. She looked up at the second floor window where her former lover sat writing at his desk, sunlight crowning his head. Had he ever missed the honey she took? Had he missed her? She stood there, willing him to feel her gaze and look up from whatever he was working on, but he never did.

2.

Sahar continued to drive well into the third year of the second American occupation. By then, her children had grown. Jamal was studying literature in Michigan. Leila was doing her best at the local university. Her mother-in-law and Saddam Hussein were dead. Sahar had given up smoking and made her own lunches. She listened to CDs instead of cassettes. As the streets grew more dangerous with craters and criminals, Qaseem begged her to stop driving, but Sahar refused to give in to the times. Her drive to and from work remained her ritual: the place where she felt most whole. To give up her car keys and hire a driver was to let the lot of them win—the Americans, the radical Shiites, Al-Qaeda, the criminals, the looters, the opportunists, the princes. So many friends and colleagues had already mutinied to the United Arab Emirates or been forced to return to their family farms. At least she was still at the museum, still "hiding its silver" as best she could, never mind that the building had been looted and the galleries closed for the past twelve years.

After a long hiatus, she'd taken another lover: an Italian bachelor ten years her junior who was developing a virtual tour of the museum. Sahar saw him only during his infrequent visits to Iraq. They communicated in English. In fact, it had been her latent desire to practice English more intimately that had led to the flirtation. Unfortunately, he was most fluent when he spoke of scans and 3-D imaging and HTML code and analytics. Qaseem knew, but refused to talk about it. This only made Sahar more defiant. Talking or not, the affair was real and splendid. Her hands sliding so easily through his thick, gelled hair. His soft lips on her neck. His uncircumcised penis.

As she cruised down the boulevard, Sahar blushed at the thought. She'd just left a museum event and felt giddy. Her keychain jangled as she swerved around the potholes created by IEDs and Humvees. The afternoon had been nearly perfect: the Assyrian Room complete and filled with diplomats and journalists for a press opening. She remembered the smashed, empty displays she'd discovered in the museum after the looting. The spilled drawers of ancient sherds, the broken vase handles, the delicate cracked necks of the sculptures. In all of this time, she'd forgotten about the energy of an opening—the gratification of seeing the objects she'd worked so hard to preserve displayed for everyone to admire.

As she presented a case of recently recovered artifacts to a small group of investors, a young man approached and asked shyly if she was Sahar Khalil. He wondered if she could help him find a gallery where he could show his work. She almost laughed at the request.

"You must have connections," the young man insisted.

"Not anymore," she answered, thinking of her brief, unrealized attraction to a sculptor with a Dali moustache. "I'm a conservator, not a curator."

Art, at least the legitimate sale of it, was one of the first things to go during a war. She felt sorry for the young man, the way she was sorry whenever her daughter Leila couldn't go to the university because of some crisis. Their generation was suffering and it wasn't because of their own doing.

"But, you knew my uncle," the young man insisted, saying a name she did not recognize. She grew leery of him. Everyone had a scam these days. Kidnappings. Blackmail. Even the museum looters had the nerve to ask for ransom before returning the artifacts they'd stolen. From one corner of the room, Leila watched her. In another, the Italian was speaking with an A.P. journalist. Sahar excused herself, but didn't know which way to turn.

The traffic lights at the intersections were down. Honking cars bullied their way through, ignoring the police officers on their stands. Sahar settled into the slow pace, trying to figure out how she could have known the young man's uncle. She realized she'd forgotten to give her condolences or ask his name. She slid in a CD and then rolled down her window to breathe in the wet air. At the next stalled intersection, a machine gun nudged its way through the window. In the moment that it took Sahar to understand, three men had climbed into the backseat of her car. Each wore a keffiyeh wrapped around his face.

"Drive," the one in the middle instructed.

Sahar gripped the wheel, continuing straight. The guy in the middle reached through the two front seats to the glove box. When it opened, a Barbra Streisand disk fell into his hand. He threw it out the window in disgust. The guy with the gun scolded him for tossing something they could have sold. After they went through Sahar's purse, the gunman poked the barrel into her neck.

"How much are you worth?" he asked.

The question overwhelmed Sahar. Even if she had an answer, she wasn't sure she could speak.

The gunman jabbed her again, this time in the shoulder blade, and repeated himself, "How much are you worth?"

Sahar shook her head as tears began to stream down her face. "I don't know. Just take the car. I won't report it missing," she said between sobs.

"Take off your earrings," he said. "And the bracelet."

At the next intersection, the men forced her out of the car and left her on a corner in a part of Baghdad she did not know. How could one measure a life's worth, Sahar wondered as she wrapped her arms around herself, remembering the blood money that she and Qaseem had prepared for the family after she'd hit the boy at the gas station those years ago. Even then, she understood that it was a valueless gesture. She remembered the thud, her eyes meeting his briefly through the windshield, the devastation she'd felt after pulling over and throwing up on the sidewalk. In her purse, the stolen honey had spilled.

As rain began to fall, the dog smell of her damp sweater reminded her that she needed to find a way home.

After the carjacking, Sahar stopped driving. The desire was gone, the thrill replaced with doubt. When it was convenient, she let Qaseem drive her to work in his car. Other times she hired a driver as she'd once sworn she would never do.

So, on the afternoon that the authorities called to say they had Leila in a morgue at the edge of Shorjah market, it felt strange for Sahar to be back in the driver's seat again. In the few months off the road, she'd lost her confidence. To avoid roadblocks, she crossed the river and then turned up Sinak Bridge near the Old City, giving no thought to the professor. For several blocks, an American convoy tailed her close until one of the soldiers said something through a loudspeaker and Sahar realized that they wanted her to pull over to let them pass. The American accents were so difficult at times, so twangy and slurred, too slow. After the Americans, she got lost. She didn't know this part of the city and with the recent sectarian fighting, routes had changed. She was distracted. Her daughter had been missing almost 24 hours.

Sahar knew she should have called Qaseem, who was already in the city center looking for their daughter. She was exhausted from the slow passing of time and needed to do something, even if it was tending to a misunderstanding. She didn't want to worry Qaseem over a cruel bureaucratic error. They knew no one in this area and Sahar was pretty sure that Leila didn't either. She would view the body, let them know it was not her daughter, and get home in time to greet Qaseem. He'd left the car for just this situation. Before leaving, Sahar wrote a quick, scolding note for Leila to find if she returned while Sahar was still out.

Sahar registered at the front desk of the morgue. The clerk got on a walkie-talkie and a young American led her toward the back of the building.

"Do you need a translator?" he asked in oddly-accented Arabic. She suspected that women rarely came into this space.

"I lived in England as a girl," Sahar answered.

The soldier spoke again into the radio clipped to his shoulder. A set of doors opened automatically. Another soldier joined him there. On another day, she might have asked if either of them were from

Michigan, where her son lived, but she was too nervous. She'd seen images of mass graves, bodies laid out in vast tents, wrapped in linen like valuable artifacts. Human shards. Even though she was sure they did not have her daughter, they had someone's and she would be seeing her soon.

The morgue was a cold room with metal doors all around and a metal table in the middle. Narrow caskets lined the walls. Only one of the overhead lights flickered on. Sahar pulled her sweater around her. One of the soldiers checked a list, then kneeled down to find the correct box. When he located the identity number he was looking for, he and the other soldier lifted the box onto the table. Dread overcame Sahar.

"Wait," she said. "What happened exactly?"

"A suicide bomber got scared, we think, and abandoned a bomb near the Shorjah market."

"Who?"

"Al-Qaeda, we presume," the other soldier answered with disgust.

"I see," Sahar said, relieved. Sunnis wouldn't kill other Sunnis. Besides, there was absolutely no reason why Leila would be so far off her usual path.

"Are you sure you don't want to wait for someone to be with you?" the soldier asked.

"There's been a mistake. Stolen identification or something. This should only take a second. My daughter would have no reason to be in this part of the city."

"Are you ready then?"

Sahar nodded. The Americans lifted the dirty sheet that had been resting on the corpse's face, folding it below the chin. She could feel them watching her as she forced herself to lower her eyes. She couldn't breathe. One of the Americans braced her.

"Don't touch me," she hissed.

She forced herself to look again, squelching the scream that burned in her throat, the food in her gut that threatened to come back up.

The face was Leila's, she could not deny it, but Leila did not have bruises like these. Her cheeks were pinker. More full. Leila never covered her beautiful hair with a shayla. It didn't make sense. Sahar summoned the courage to pull the sheet down a bit further, seeking out more differences, an explanation, a way to understand. But there was no way to deny that this was her daughter.

Sahar lifted the battered hand. Leila would never be a nurse, a doctor, a surgeon. Never travel abroad. Never love or marry. Never bring a glass of tea to her lips again. She touched her daughter's cheek, her lips. How thirsty she must be. Even as everything inside Sahar crumbled and dissolved, a voice in her head told her to remain calm. She wouldn't wail. She wouldn't beat her chest. She wouldn't cry out. She needed to get home before Qaseem, but first she needed to be with Leila. She turned to the soldier and requested a bucket of water and some time alone with the body.

"The least I can do is wash this girl for her family," she explained.

The soldiers looked at each other and then complied.

Alone, Sahar undressed Leila and then began to wash her bruised and broken body, starting at her feet, reciting the words of the Rumi poem once again. "This is love," she began. When she was done, she took the identification and left her daughter's body unclaimed.

MISUNDERSTANDINGS

SINCE RETURNING from Iraq, Clark was constantly reminded of how it felt to be a child—his parents' bodies elongated and hovering, their gestures unreadable. His mother's concerned eyes, he remembered, rarely meant she was listening. Nor had his father's silence indicated a lack of something to say. Clark had assumed he was the one to misunderstand. Now, he knew better. Lost, that's how it had felt to be a child, lost and illiterate, destined to trust.

He remembered the day distinctly. This was years ago, during the first Gulf War. Clark was too young for school. His father was in Saudi Arabia, his grandmother dying in a hospital, and his mother lugging him along behind her wherever she went like a suitcase she would never stop to unpack.

He and his mother had made their way from the slushy parking lot to the sidewalk leading to the hospital doors. Salt pebbles rolled under his rubber soles with each step. There was a game he liked to play: When Will Daddy Be Home? When in the mood, his mother played along, inventing new answers: lilac season, in time for the World Series, Bloomsday, when Lolo is well again, when we forget his face, when you graduate from college. Clark knew that no matter what she said, the real answer would stay the same: May 24. Two more pages to flip on the calendar by the phone. Clark would still be four years old. It would be spring.

Today, his mother's answer was a tug on the hand. "Move a little faster, Clark. We're late."

They were always late, his mother always rushing. Clark rarely understood why. No matter what time they arrived at the hospital, his grandmother was always resting in her bed, not having gone anywhere. The thought of the boredom to come made him tired. He held his arms up to his mother and she hoisted him up. He rode her hip as best he could. When she bounced him back up, his testicles got squished and he had to wiggle himself free. First one boot, then the other fell to the sidewalk. His mother bent to pick them up, letting out a heavy sigh.

At the entrance, she stepped onto the mat and the doors opened. With a twinge of regret, Clark realized triggering the automated doors was something he liked to do. He hung onto her shoulders tighter, sucking on a strand of her hair as they rushed by the hospital's interesting things—the candy baskets and gift shop bears, the sleeping people who seemed to levitate in the air, and the drooping patients in wheelchairs, their liquid-filled bags floating above them like comic strip captions.

His grandmother was one of those people, tired and thin, her eyes milky, her skin the same pale gray as the hospital floors. Her breath smelled like old Band-Aids. Clark stood at arm's length. Two hospital balloons always hovered above her bed. One was filled with clear liquid, the other with a pinkish liquid. They had tubes that were taped to his grandmother's arm as if they might float away. What was inside these bags either kept her alive or was killing her. He'd overheard the adults say both—Loretta is in the hospital to get better; Loretta is in the hospital to die.

Loretta, he figured out, was his grandmother's name. He'd always called her Lolo and she'd always answered to that.

He and his mother stopped at the semi-circular counter where the nurses greeted visitors. His mother set him down to pull a tin of green cookies from her purse, apologizing that they were store-bought and probably a little crumbled. She squeezed his shoulders. You shouldn't have, the nurses usually said, patting their hips or bellies or behinds. That day, it was a nurse named Kusla, and she wasn't smiling.

"How is she?" his mother asked.

"No one called?"

"We've been on the road. What's happened?"

And then the weight of his mother's hand on his shoulder was gone. Her hand was not on him at all or even hovering within reach. Clark looked down the long white corridor where she was rushing away from him, sobbing, her hand trailing slightly behind her, open, as if she were scattering seeds. Was she pretending he was there? Stop, he thought, but did not say. He ducked behind a cart and let himself disappear.

Looking back, he couldn't be sure why he did this. Was he trying to test his mother? Was he glad for the distance, the freedom of being entirely forgotten? Whatever it was, the reason never took hold, merely the image of her leaving. Clark could remember feeling like he might have to pee. Too often he forgot to listen to his body, as his mother scolded. He closed his eyes and listened: Do I have to pee? No. Maybe. He remembered the glass of water he'd insisted on at the last minute and the huge sigh his mother made before she tromped off to the kitchen to fill his car cup. Thirst was one thing she could not deny. He felt a pressure beneath his belly button. He slid down against the white wall and landed on his butt, rocking back and forth until the pee-urge went away.

When the nearby elevator opened, Clark pushed himself up and hurried inside. He would go to the bathroom on his own—like a big boy. His mother would be pleased. When he put his hands in his pocket, he found a nickel and a dime, treasures retrieved from the car. This gave him a new idea. He would go to the basement cafeteria, grab a tray, and try the butterscotch pudding his uncle once discouraged him from taking. He knew the way.

On the next floor, a doctor got in and gave him a wink. The doctor's head and shoes were covered with blue shower caps, his coat splattered with red. Blood! Clark positioned himself next to a grandmother holding a bouquet of yellow flowers and closed his eyes as the elevator started to drop again. He wondered what Kusla, her stethoscope dangling out of her front pocket like a pet snake, had said to his mother. Was his grandmother angry with them for being late? He wondered what his mother would do when she discovered that he was missing. A part of him knew to go back, but he didn't.

When the elevator doors opened, Clark stepped into the busy, familiar corridor outside the cafeteria. A cart of rattling little cups nearly knocked him over. "I'm sorry, darling," said a voice that kept going. He automatically reached up for his mother's hand and then remembered he was alone. He thought about his father in Saudi Arabia—how people said he was brave. It was this that must have propelled him forward.

When Clark entered the cafeteria, the pink-cheeked cashier greeted him with a "Hi, honey." Like all of the old ladies who worked in the kitchen, she wore a spider web over her hair.

At the buffet line, Clark slid a tray along the metal counter. The first time his grandmother had stayed in the hospital he and his uncle had been regulars, trying the different foods one-by-one like scientists. Here, all food had the same name as it did at home, except he and his uncle put the word hospital in front of it. Clark had hospital soup, hospital Jell-O, hospital fries that his uncle dipped in ranch dressing, and hospital hot cocoa that came from a machine. After lunch they both chewed on toothpicks and talked about Clark's dad and what he might have been doing at that exact moment in Saudi Arabia. And then just about the time that his grandmother went back into the hospital, his uncle and mother had one of their misunderstandings, as his grandmother called them. Now, his uncle waited in the lobby for them to leave and Clark had no one to talk to about his father.

Clark pointed to the caramel-colored pudding with its dollop of whipped cream and a neon-red cherry on top. The lady behind the counter set the pudding up on the top of the glass where he couldn't reach it. Clark stood patiently until the person behind him set the cup onto his tray and gave him a nudge. From the open refrigerator, Clark took a small carton of chocolate milk. At the register, he held out his hand with the fifteen cents and the pink-cheeked lady told him it was on the house. He stood there smiling, waiting for her to push the buttons on the cash register until she folded his hand over his coins and shooed him away.

He thought of his mother. She would not want him here. But why? He considered his tray of food. He could eat it and return before she ever noticed he was gone. He crossed the wide room of tables and chairs toward the wall of booths where he and his uncle used to sit. Carefully balancing the tray with its two items and a spoon, Clark climbed up onto the bench and took the first bite. The pudding was sweet and tasted like brown sugar. Delicious. One of the only things in his life that had actually met his expectations. He savored it as he looked out the cafeteria windows onto the snowy lawn that made the room feel like an igloo. When they'd come to the hospital for the first time, leaves were piled against the windows. Clark's father was still home.

In the weeks before he shipped off, he took Clark everywhere— to the hardware store to buy a new dryer vent, to an Indians baseball game at the big stadium, to the railroad office to submit paperwork, to Shagnasty's for fries and apple juice and peanuts with shells that they cracked and threw directly onto the floor.

The restaurant had a bad, wet-dog smell. The dining room, where they sat, was empty and all but forgotten by the servers. Everyone else sat in the loud, dark bar. Through the narrow doorway, he could see his uncle Frederick sitting on a barstool, talking to the bartender. He looked off-center, as if he were seated on one of the yellow horses on springs in the park. Clark couldn't help but wonder if it smelled any better in there. From across the table, Clark's father raised his beer and clinked Clark's apple juice glass.

"I'm going to miss you, son," he said.

Clark gulped his apple juice. His father called him Clark and kid and Dibs. Never son. He shuffled through the basket of stringy peanut shell remains, most of which concealed the single nuts that his fingers could not retrieve.

His father cleared his throat. "I'll be back before you know it."

His father kept repeating the same things over and over.

"I love you, Dibs."

Clark nodded. They sat in silence and then his father said it again. "I love you, kid."

"Don't say that anymore," Clark said.

His father licked a dab of beer foam from his upper lip. "But it's true."

"But I already know that. You already told me."

"I'm making up for all the days I won't be able to tell you in person."

"But I'm tired of you telling me that."

Clark's father looked down, nodding his head in agreement. "OK," he finally said. "I'll lay off the gushy stuff for a while."

His father grabbed the last handful of peanuts and began to crack them for Clark, handing them over so quickly that Clark couldn't keep up. Eventually, the bartender arrived with a platter of fries. Uncle Frederick came in and slid into the wooden booth alongside Clark, patting him too hard on the back, the way he always did. Clark coughed, the inside of his mouth paper dry from all of the peanuts he'd eaten. His fingertips and lips burned from the salt.

His father's hair was still bushy then. Before they left, he swept it up and then placed his baseball cap on top. Days later his father flew out: beige fatigues tucked into his boots, hair buzzed short, his head surprisingly square. Whenever an airplane passed over them, Clark looked up and waved. But his father was not in an airplane, his mother had explained more than once. "He's landed now, Clark. He's on another continent, in another day and time."

"Is he sleeping?" Clark asked.

"Dreaming of you," his mother would say, touching his hair tenderly.

In the cafeteria, Clark continued to shovel spoonfuls of pudding into his mouth, shaping them with his lips, sucking the creamy sweetness over his tongue. When he looked up, Don was smiling down at him.

Don was a nurse like Kusla. He wore bright-yellow T-shirts under his white coat and white shoes with springs in the heels that made him even taller than he already was. He was as big as Clark's uncle but completely different in every other way. He had long, silvery hair that made him look like God in the ceiling paintings his mother sometimes showed him in the giant art book she had. He never raised his voice above a whisper or raced down the hall like the other nurses.

"May I?" he asked, before sliding in across the table from Clark.

Clark happily nodded yes. He and Don had good conversations. Once when the tube had clogged on his grandmother's arm, Clark watched as Don slid the needle into her wrinkly skin as if he were mending her. Another time, he let Clark listen through his stethoscope to his own heartbeat. Hearing the impatient tapping, Clark had finally understood what his mother meant about listening to his body. When Clark's uncle called Don a fairy, his mother rolled her eyes in disagreement and scolded him. But Clark had agreed, Don had special powers.

The doctors were always comparing his grandmother's tumors to fruits or different sports balls, making it difficult for Clark to picture them. Clark asked Don what he thought.

"They all look different depending on where they're located, what kind of cells they're reproducing. Does that make sense? In general, I'd say they look like fungi."

"Fungi?" Clark asked.

"Weird mushrooms. They get big and then most of them split and then those get bigger and bigger and split again, taking on different shapes."

"Like clouds?"

"Like clouds. I like that. I guess you could say cancer is a kind of storm building up inside the body."

Clark imagined the storm inside Lolo. At the bottom of her body close to the bed were the low hills made up of her bones and organs, each day more of it obscured by dark cancer clouds. That would explain the circles under her eyes, how cold her fingers had become. He thought of his father again, his airplane suspended over the shapes, hidden in those clouds. Clark worried that he was lost.

"Where's your mom?" Don asked, blowing on his coffee.

"With Loretta," Clark said.

"You're not here on your own, are you?" Don looked worried.

"She's coming," Clark lied.

"How's your grandmother today?" Don asked.

His quiet voice reminded Clark of the way his father's voice sounded when he woke Clark in the mornings, when it was still dark outside.

"Good," Clark lied again, reassured that Don had not been upstairs. Yesterday Lolo had called Clark her little man and let him push the buttons on her bed to raise it to a sitting position. "She's looking ready to come home," Clark ventured.

"They say she won't, Clark," Don said, his voice not changing. The coffee steam floated across the table to Clark.

"She'll live here forever?"

"As long as she's alive. But, she doesn't have much time. She's dying."

"I know."

"Do you know what that means?" Don raised his eyebrows.

Clark had seen death: the trail of expired ants after his mother sprayed under the kitchen sink, the skunks and porcupines and once even a small deer on the side of the road, the mouse tails that the cat left by their kitchen door. He thought of his grandmother on a gurney, a sheet pulled over her head like a victim in the cop shows his uncle let him watch when he used to babysit. Clark held Don's gaze, and then drew a line across his neck as he stuck out his tongue.

Don smiled and put his hand on Clark's arm. "It's not usually so extreme as that. It's more like sleep." He paused. "Except when you die, you don't wake up."

"Snow White woke up," Clark corrected, taking another big, delicious bite of pudding.

Don nodded. "With death nothing can wake you. Not even a prince."

"Do you stop dreaming too?" Clark asked, thinking of his father.

Don shook his head and looked toward the door. "Depends on who you ask, I suppose. What do you think?"

Clark shrugged.

Don smiled. "How is your mother holding up?"

"OK, I guess." Clark sucked in another spoonful of pudding, swallowed, and then blurted out, "Do you have kids?"

When he'd asked his mother the same question about Don, she'd shaken her head and explained that it was impolite to ask personal questions.

"Not that I know of," Don answered with a chuckle.

The idea baffled Clark. How could a dad not know if he had kids?

"You miss your dad, don't you?" Don asked.

Clark nodded.

"Me too. I haven't talked to mine in over ten years."

The two of them sat for a while. Don showed Clark how to drink milk directly from the carton. Clark offered a bit of the chocolate for Don's coffee. His uncle drank it that way sometimes. Sitting in this quiet was the sort of thing that Clark would do with his father, but not his uncle who was talkative, his words often looping and difficult to follow, slipping out of the lines the same way Clark's crayons did in the coloring book.

"Remind me, when is your dad coming home?" Don finally asked.

"May 24," Clark answered.

"This is a hard time for your mom to be alone."

"I'm with her," Clark said.

"True enough," Don nodded.

They sat there again in silence, the sun warming up the side of Clark's face. Outside, the once-deep footprints were melting into odd shapes.

Don looked at his watch. "It looks like your mom might have gotten caught up in something. Can I take you back?"

Clark was grateful for the invitation, but when he went to slide out of the booth, he realized he'd done it again: stopped listening to his body. He began to cry.

Confused by Clark's sudden burst of emotion, Don kneeled, pulling Clark into his arms to let him know that his grandmother would be in less pain when she died. This only made Clark cry louder. Finally Don pulled away and looked at Clark's face and then the widening wet circle in the front of his pants.

"Uh oh," he said, and then even more gently than usual, "This can be fixed. This is just temporary." He lifted Clark into his arms, not at all worried about getting himself wet.

Don's long, bouncy stride reminded Clark of when his father came home from work and lifted Clark up, swinging him in the air so that his limbs propelled like a sprinkler. Clark reached behind Don's head to the ponytail and grasped it the same way he did his mother's hair, although he did not put it in his mouth. Don patted Clark's back and whispered, "Just a quick detour."

When they stepped out of the elevator, they were on a new floor that Clark had not known about all of this time, one with bright-blue whale posters in the hallway and a room filled with toys. Inside, three children—two of them bald—played with a train track, but Don whisked Clark by all of this and through a locked door.

The fluorescent flicker revealed a disappointing storage room with plain cement walls lined with metal shelves loaded with boxes and plastic storage bins. Don studied the labels and then pulled a large disposable diaper from one of the bins before setting Clark down on the floor. The wetness in Clark's pants was simultaneously warm and cold. He watched as Don pulled used clothes from another box on a low shelf and held them up to Clark for size: a pair of red stretchy girl's leggings and then tiny sweatpants.

"Where should we do this?" Don asked when he'd found a pair of overalls that would fit.

Clark didn't say anything. He was looking at the shelves of tiny pink tubs and stacks of blue and pink hospital gowns, the boxes and boxes of blue gloves. Once Kusla had blown one up into a frilly rooster head.

"Here's as good as anywhere I guess," Don finally said.

Resting on his knees, he helped Clark out of his boots, wet pants, and underpants, and gave Clark a baby blanket to pat himself dry. He wadded up Clark's wet clothes, slid them into a blue plastic bag and opened the diaper. "Can you do this yourself?" he asked.

Clark straddled the diaper and held up the front, but after taping one side, it was lopsided. "Teamwork," Don said as he readjusted the tape.

Clark hugged Don gratefully and then kissed him on the cheek just as his father had done at the airport. Don returned the hug, patting his back. Then, did Clark say them or just think the words I love you? No matter, something shifted in the room.

Don stood quickly, knocking Clark off balance. Shaking his head, he said, "What was I thinking? Let's get this over with." He held out the overalls with his arms stiffly stretched in front of him, avoiding Clark's eyes.

Confused, Clark climbed into the loose legs and pulled up the straps. One of the buckles was missing, so they hung crooked on him. "Good enough," Don said, already at the door. He stuck his head out, looked both ways, and then rushed them down the hall.

In the elevator, Don pushed a floor number without saying anything. He seemed nervous and far away. He lifted his white jacket and sniffed at the damp area where Clark had pressed against him. This time, when Clark reached his hand up for Don's, the nurse didn't take it. Clark's cheeks went hot, but the rest of him was cold and sad.

"I won't tell," Clark offered. It was the sort of thing that sometimes comforted his mother.

This only made things worse. "There is absolutely nothing to tell," Don answered quietly. "Do you understand, Clark?"

Clark nodded, completely confused. When the door opened, he followed Don to the half-moon counter and watched as Don smiled his usual friendly way at Kusla and took a cookie from the green tin. "Look who I found wandering the premises."

Not much later, Clark's mother stepped out from the stairwell. She wasn't alone. Uncle Frederick followed, patting her shoulder, telling her to be calm. It was strange, considering the two of them had barely spoken since Clark's grandmother had been re-admitted to the hospital. Clark slid behind Don hoping they wouldn't see him.

No such luck. His uncle saw him first and got his mother's attention. When her eyes landed on Clark, she screamed his name and ran to him, kneeling down and squeezing him so tight he could not breathe. Her tears were hot and wet against his cheek. "I've been frantic, looking everywhere. Where have you been?" Clark had no time to answer before his mother began to shake him, her voice growing angry. "Don't you ever do that again. Do you hear me? I've been going out of my mind."

From over her shoulder, Clark watched Don and Kusla exchange glances. "Jen, he was safe. He was here with me. Right, Don?"

"He had an accident. Kusla took him to the children's ward and changed him."

"Of all days, Clark. Really?" she asked, her hands on either side of his shoulders.

Everyone was looking at him, yet he felt invisible.

"Now, it's time to say goodbye to Loretta," Kusla said quietly. "Why doesn't Clark stay with Don while I take you and your brother to her room?"

"I need Clark with me," his mother said, holding her hand out for his.

Clark looked from his mother over to Don, who had dropped into a lobby chair near the nurse's station. He'd removed his damp jacket, and held it in his lap. The bag with Clark's wet pants sat limp at his feet. His long hair was hidden behind him, so that he looked to Clark like an ordinary man. Not a fairy. Not a god. Clark ran to him.

AMNESTY

NALAH SAT in the backseat hugging her purse to her bosom to stop the jiggle, a sensation that made her feel unmoored. Every bump in the street—which her daughter-in-law Sahar was so skilled at finding—ignited the chronic pain in Nalah's jaw, sending it further up alongside her ear and into her skull, like a nail being hammered in. Outside the window, Baghdad was busy with morning: cars honking, a man dressing a mannequin in a boutique window, women pulling uniformed children along the sidewalk, young men weaving through the traffic on rickety bicycles, two men pasting a poster of President Hussein high up on a billboard.

In the seat next to Nalah, Leila, her twenty-year-old granddaughter, began another inquisition. Nalah couldn't help but associate the girl's questions with the excruciating pain in her jaw. The two together were becoming intolerable.

"Who is this friend you are visiting?" her granddaughter asked.

"An old friend," Nalah said without looking at Leila. Nalah thought not of Salim, the young man she hoped to find at Abu Ghraib prison, but of his mother Hayfa, a childhood friend who had once been her confidant. There was a time when she'd known every detail of the woman's life. Over a year ago, Nalah had heard that Hayfa had died.

"Why haven't you visited her before?"

"Stop pestering me, Leila."

Yesterday on the government news channel, President Hussein promised to open the doors to the prison to let the inmates free. The idea sent a chill through Nalah. She imagined the dark, dank cells where car thieves were packed in with military deserters, murderers with the devout. She wondered if the victims' and perpetrators' starved, grimy faces, blinking in the new light, would all look the same. On the television, a family wept and sang, praising Saddam Hussein, although it was because of him that their son, a classic case of wrong place, wrong time, had been in the prison for four years. This was the same for Salim, except he'd been in prison seventeen years. If she didn't go, would there be anyone to greet him?

Nalah noticed a bakery two blocks ahead. "There," she yelled out, pointing toward it. "Pull over, please."

"We're not even close," Sahar complained from the driver's seat, putting on her blinker without slowing.

"I need to buy sweets for the visit."

"Oh, I love kleicha. What kind will you get? Date? Rose water? You should be careful of the sugars, of course. I could help you choose." On and on. Leila was so interested in others, so obsessed about health. She would make a lovely wife for an older man if she'd only get over her idea of becoming a doctor. Nalah couldn't understand why a young woman would want to spend a decade in school looking at cadavers.

"There's got to be a bakery closer to where we're taking you," Sahar suggested. "The traffic won't be so bad."

"I'll take a cab the rest of the way. I'm making you late for work."

"Mother, let me drive you. It is no trouble and it will be nice to see your old neighborhood."

"Stop the car, daughter-in-law," Nalah said, pounding her fist in her lap.

With this, Sahar obeyed, swerving into an open space two doors in front of the bakery. The car behind them honked. Nalah slid out curbside and slammed the door. She stood for a moment, making sure that her purse was zipped, her coat straight, and her scarf in place. From the idling car, Sahar and Leila watched for her to enter the bakery. Knowing the two of them, they would still be there when she walked back out with the bag of cookies. Taking sweets to a prison was absurd, as was asking a bakery for an empty bag. Her jaw hurt so much; she couldn't imagine taking even a bite of kleicha. She closed her eyes to soothe the pain. Opening them again, she turned in the opposite direction of the bakery and began to walk. Leila yelled out of her window, "Grandmamma," but Nalah pretended not to hear. Deafness, her mother had told her before she died, was one of the gifts of old age. Nalah imagined Leila and Sahar dumbfounded in the car, watching her grow smaller, arguing about what to do next. This made her smile. The smile made her pain worse. She turned a corner so she would disappear faster.

As she walked, Nalah thought of her son, Youssef. If he had been caught and imprisoned instead of Salim, at least he, too, would be freed today. She would know where he was and could see him again. Nalah tried to imagine the two of them looking at each other across all of that lost time—the hugs and weeping, the emphatic way in which he'd always said, "Mama." She would take him in her arms and say, "Son, you are home." Although she hadn't spoken the words out loud, another pain shot up her jaw.

The cab, which took Nalah twenty minutes to hail and was double the usual fare, dropped her off in front of the prison's main gates where an eager mass of people slowly funneled through. Nalah clutched her purse. Tucked in the lining was all of the money she had left from her husband's savings. She'd overheard her other son Qaseem say to Sahar one evening that it was the equivalent of two college educations abroad, or at least enough to get them started. Offended that they spoke as if the money were already theirs, Nalah had withdrawn it from the bank the very next day and hidden it inside a box of perfumed powder. Up until yesterday, she hadn't known what she would do with it. Now in her purse, the bills emitted the scent of a freshly bathed infant.

No one spoke of Youssef anymore, yet not a day went by when Nalah didn't yearn for her youngest son, the single person in her family who had ever needed her. After he left Iraq, she received only one letter from him, postmarked Syria, asking her to wire money to an account. She continued to wire large sums to the account each month, eagerly checking her bank statements to be sure it had been received. She never allowed herself to imagine the worst. Instead, she thought of him buying the simple things he needed: a toothbrush, a newspaper, a bag of kleicha for a wife, or maybe a toy for a baby. What she had in her purse could buy just this—the beginnings of a modest life.

A bus pulled up and another wave of people rushed toward the gate. She turned to see if her cab was still there and was nearly pushed down. A garbled voice in the speaker system announced something about cell blocks. Nalah realized she didn't know which block Hayfa's son was in or if there were other entry-points and lines for her to join. She was lost. The thought made her frightened and strangely giddy, as if she'd arrived in an unknown town without the address for the person she was visiting. The crowd's current pushed her forward. Up ahead, a ladder had been set up on top of a car chassis; chairs and crates formed makeshift stairs to its roof: a short cut. Clutching her purse, she squinted up into the October sun. At the top of the fence, several prayer carpets were laid over the cut glass. Nalah lined up and watched as another woman her age scaled the fence to the top. In her black abaya, the woman looked like a crow hunting for something bright to claim.

"Are you going?" a young man asked Nalah impatiently.

She accepted a boost onto the car roof and then placed her hands on the rungs of a ladder and began to climb until she could see into the prison grounds. Guards watched over the crowd with their rifles. Below, people milled around, calling out names. A long line had formed along the building. Nalah took hold of a rope and eased herself down into the prison, her coat catching on something sharp and ripping. How strange to be letting oneself into a prison. She tried to think of a word that meant the opposite of escape. Just as she reached the ground, the metal doors to one of the buildings opened and the ghost men began to march out, looking worse than she'd imagined. It was impossible to believe that any of them had been dangerous, that any of them had been anything at all.

A few moments later, their foul smell reached her. Nalah gagged and stumbled. A hand caught her elbow and righted her. She stepped over a guard sprawled on the ground, bleeding. If she didn't keep up, she would be trampled too. Still clinging to her purse, she gave in to the crowd's momentum. The word she had been searching for came to her: surrender. A voice from behind her yelled, "Mohammed, is that you?" Several inmates looked up toward the voice hopefully, but only one was rewarded with a familiar face. He stepped forward cautiously as a middle-aged woman broke free from the crowd and ran toward him with her arms outstretched. It was impossible to determine if he was her son, husband, or father.

Up ahead at a table, three guards shared a stapled paper list of names. Two more guards patrolled the line that disappeared around the corner of the building. Nalah's heart sank. Salim had been in prison for over a decade. She gasped at the math, the cruelty of it. She was too late: all that could be taken from him had been.

Nalah stood in the line for hours. In that time, she counted the rats circling the base of the fence she'd climbed. Her feet swelled from the heat, her jaw buzzed with pain, and her coat was too heavy and hot; she had to pee in a terrible way. When she grew dizzy, she leaned against the building and studied the faces around her. Some had been transformed by worry. Others were ecstatic with hope. Occasionally, but not as often as one might expect, a family found a loved one and the reunion was joyful. Mostly, she witnessed variations of disappointment. She had no idea what to expect when she reached the front of the line. The last time she'd seen Salim, he'd been a careless young man and Youssef's last friend. She would see him coming and going in various loud cars, a boom box in his hands. That was nearly two decades ago.

By then, Youssef had returned from the war against Iran, lame and hard of hearing, with an incompatible mix of arrogance and skittishness. At night, he called out the names of young men she did not know. Rushing into his room, she would find him sitting up in bed with his eyes open, staring at someone she could not see. She guessed whoever it was, was dead. When she tried to hold him, he lashed out at her. He'd grown up a proud Sunni, son of a Ba'ath Party official. As soon as hair had sprouted on his upper lip, he'd grown a Saddam moustache. His father bragged when he joined the Army. And bragged even more when Youssef declined easier duties in order to go to the front. When he returned home a few months later with a foot injury, his father assumed it was self-inflicted. Nothing Nalah said changed her husband's mind. He was convinced that Youssef was a coward.

Youssef was not prepared for this level of rejection. He began to spend more time away from home. For a while, she saw her son only when she visited her friend Hayfa. Hayfa lived in Kadhimiya, next to the house where Nalah had grown up. One afternoon, Nalah and Hayfa sat together in Hayfa's garden. Sunlight streamed through the glossy leaf clusters of the persimmon tree. A hummingbird sucked nectar from the naranja blossoms along their shared wall. Hayfa grew quiet. She smashed an ant that had crawled up the leg of her chair.

"How is Youssef doing?"

"I was going to ask you the same thing. I haven't set eyes on him for a few days. I thought I might see him here."

Hayfa shook her head. "My husband has asked Youssef not to return to our house," she said, reaching over to take Nalah's hand.

Nalah was saddened to consider yet another loss for her son. "Oh, dear, are he and Salim fighting? I will speak with him."

"My husband is firm."

"But what has he done?"

Hayfa shook her head. "He is saying dangerous things about the president. His behavior is—erratic."

Several of Hayfa's daughters stepped out into the garden, so deep into a sibling squabble that they didn't notice the two women. Nalah pulled her hand out from under Hayfa's. The smell of the blooms on her friend's naranja tree had become so sweet that Nalah thought she might retch. All their lives, it hadn't mattered that Hayfa was a Shia and Nalah a Sunni. They were like sisters, even after they married and Nalah moved across the Tigris to Adhamiyah. Their children had grown up together like cousins. Hayfa was accusing her son of being a heretic, or worse, a lunatic.

Nalah could no longer look her friend in the eye. After that day, she vowed never to return to Hayfa's garden and asked her parents' gardener to prune the naranja that grew over the side of their shared wall.

It took Nalah nearly five hours to find herself face-to-face with one of the guards holding the list.

"Inmate number," he demanded.

"I'm sorry, I don't have one."

"Name?"

She said Salim's full name and waited, worried that the guard would ask for paperwork she didn't have or that her jaw would refuse to move.

He sighed with annoyance and grabbed another list. "Crime?"

"Car theft."

"Year?"

"1985."

"Ah, here he is," the guard finally said, pointing his finger at the paper and looking up at her. "Says here he was an enemy of the state."

Nalah smiled dumbly.

"What's your relationship?"

"Aunt. His parents have passed away."

"His cell block opened two hours ago," he speculated, looking at his watch. "You can see if he's still there in the waiting area."

He handed her a yellow slip of paper and gestured toward a fenced-in yard where small clusters of unclaimed prisoners sat under the hot sun. Nalah thanked the man and then wondered why. It was well past three o'clock. She didn't see a way to get to the other side, but the guard was already speaking to another family who had begun to wail.

After walking the length of the fence, Nalah eventually found an opening and slipped through it, the rip in her coat opening further. Clutching the torn seam, she looked around. The space reminded her of images she'd seen of refugee camps. Where would all of these freed men go tonight if no one came to claim them? Nalah began walking from group to group, slowly studying each face before turning to the next. If Salim were among them, he would be easy to find. Salim, the youngest of Hayfa's children, had been a fair child. A distant Kurdish gene Hayfa speculated when his hair came in nearly blond, joking about her husband's dismay. As she spoke, she smiled down at the child pulling himself up using the legs of her chair. "Our Christian baby, even born near their prophet's birthday," she said, lifting him to her lap.

Men looked up eagerly as Nalah passed by. If she looked into the eyes of a murderer, would she know? The innocent and petty criminals had been freed, but surely some of these men were the guilty ones, the violent and depraved. Freeing them was certainly not amnesty as the president was referring to it, but calculated anarchy. Men like Saddam did not forgive. Nalah understood this, because she'd been married to such a man. And in the process, she had become such a woman.

Just as Nalah was about to give up, she came upon a man with light-brown hair sprinkled with gray. He sat alone, his forehead resting on his knees. Plastic sandals revealed black, calloused feet. His clothes hung on his gaunt body. His folded shirtsleeves revealed a pocked path of cigarette burns making their way up his arms.

As she got closer, she spoke his name. "Salim?"

He looked up, his green eyes squinting at her.

"Are you Salim?" she asked again slowly.

He thought for a moment and then spoke cautiously. "Yes, but who are you?" He was missing several teeth.

"Mrs. Khalil, from next door."

"Is Youssef here?" he asked in surprise.

"Your mother sent me," Nalah answered, offering him a bottle of water she'd bought from a hawker for five times the usual price. He unscrewed the cap and drank it down as if afraid she might change her mind and take it from him. When he was done, he replied, "But she's dead."

Nalah held out her hand to help him up. When she handed him his pardoning papers, he looked at them and then said loud enough for the guards to hear, "Praise Saddam, most benevolent. I am free."

They rode side by side in the backseat of a cab toward Kadhimiya. A predominantly Shia neighborhood, it was a busy, cosmopolitan area where Sunni and Shiite families lived side by side, identifying more as Arabs than by religious sect. Their arguments with each other were intellectual, not ideological. They married each other and celebrated holidays together, their lives more or less the same. Now in preparation for an American invasion, duct tape crisscrossed the large windows. Storefronts were boarded shut, streets barricaded, and windows shuttered. The people with enough money or relatives in the country were already gone.

Nalah remembered the last time she'd seen Hayfa. Nalah had been helping her siblings with the family house after her mother died. From her parents' threshold, Nalah instructed men lugging boxes to a white truck. When Hayfa came out of her home, the two neighbors exchanged glances. Neither had spoken honestly to the other in almost five years. It was clear that each was waiting for the other to speak. A town car pulled up and Hayfa was gone. By then, they were both old women: widows and grandmothers. Neither would see her youngest son again. Nalah heard that Hayfa died soon after that day.

Beside Nalah, Salim remained silent, his face opaque. What could the young man be thinking? Feeling? She reached over and took his hand, imagining taking him home with her, preparing dolmas and grilled meats. She could use the money in her purse to get his life started again. Only once, when a sports car drove by, did she hear him breathe. She wondered if he knew about the airplanes that had flown into the skyscrapers in New York, the accusations of nuclear weapons. She pointed to a man pulling a cart filled with kerosene cases and explained, "War preparations."

"Who are we fighting?" Salim asked, disinterested.

"The Americans," Nalah answered.

"Still?" he asked.

"A new generation," she answered.

When the cab stopped in front of Salim's family house, he stared out the window, but did not open the car door. Nalah wondered if he was frightened. Did he know how long he'd been away—how much could have changed? Across the street, a group of elderly men looked up from their chessboard. They were probably the same boys her brothers had played with as children.

"I hope they're home," she said as she opened the car door and led him toward his family's house.

Above them, a face peered out from a window. They could hear a squeal come from inside and feet pounding on stairs. A woman threw open the front door and wrapped her arms around Salim. She wore a tracksuit—shiny and too bright—and no head covering. Nalah recognized her as one of the middle daughters, the one whose clothing and lack of respect had made Hayfa complain. The brother and sister wept and held each other for a long time. Nalah stepped backward, thinking it was best to simply disappear. She'd delivered Salim, but would never be able to return this family to what it had been.

The young woman stopped her. "Mrs. Khalil, it's you, isn't it? I don't know how to thank you. My sisters have gone to the prison, but they weren't sure if they could find him. You must stay for tea."

The inside of the house was as cluttered with life as Nalah remembered: shoes lined the hallway by the door, toys were strewn in front of the television that was turned to the news as it always had been, fruit flies circled above a wire basket filled with golden dates and figs. Along the wall were bulk supplies: onions, kerosene for the stove. A baby crawled into the room. "This is Sermed. I help my sisters and nieces. Between them, there are ten children," Hayfa's daughter explained. She bent down to pick him up so he could touch Salim's face, but the child was afraid. "We will start the water, you should go on out to the garden," she told Nalah.

Nalah obeyed, glad for a moment to herself. She breathed in the naranja as she stepped into the garden she'd never expected to be in again, remembering a day when her two sons had played games under the trees with Hayfa's girls. Salim's light baby hair shone in the sun. Youssef, a few years older, happily built a tower of blocks and then knocked them down to make Salim laugh. And then, it seemed without any time passing, he and Youssef were young men, smoking together, playing chess or arguing about music and sports, in the back of the garden.

The day of Salim's arrest, Hayfa came to Nalah's home in Adhamiyah. The two women sat on cushions in the living room, sharing pomegranate seeds. For an hour, their friendship picked up where it had left off. Nalah thought Hayfa was there to apologize.

"You seem sad today," Nalah offered.

"The police have Salim."

"Oh?"

"He was caught with your husband's car," Hayfa said regretfully.

Nalah was surprised. Her husband had not mentioned that the car had gone missing. Still, she understood her friend's disappointment, her humiliation. She wanted to show Hayfa that her family could be more generous to her son than Hayfa's had been to hers. "Surely he intended to return it."

"It's not so simple."

"We will not press charges. I will make sure of that."

"Oh, thank you," Hayfa said, her tears beginning to flow. "He is so reckless. When the police called, we half-expected it to be a car accident."

"He's OK?"

Hayfa nodded. "He was pulled over for speeding, but when the police officers searched the car, they found the pamphlets in the trunk."

"Pamphlets?"

"Surely you know—forbidden teachings, photographs of Mohammed Bakr al-Sadr."

"Salim too?" Nalah asked, sadly.

Hayfa shook her head, the hopefulness in her voice dropping away as she spoke. "They weren't his. Salim didn't even know they were there or what they were, but he didn't want to admit that the car was stolen so when the police asked, he said yes."

"But whose were they then?" Nalah asked.

Hayfa stood, looking down at her feet as she walked to the door. "I will understand your decision either way."

Nalah never had a chance to make a decision. Even as the two women spoke, Nalah's husband was at the police station. His actions that day—the lies, the charges against Salim—surely saved her own son's life. The pamphlets in the car proved that Youssef had turned his back not only on the president, but also on his family. Whatever had happened at the border to the young men whose names her son called out had changed him more deeply than Nalah could fathom. Still, she couldn't forgive her husband for his actions and the way they'd hurt Hayfa's family.

Salim's sister stepped out into the garden with the tea and a box of date biscuits. Salim followed quietly, looking around with a dazed disbelief. Nalah wondered if he, too, could feel Hayfa's presence. Even with all of the suffering that had happened here, the good remained.

"What about you, Mrs. Khalil? You must be a grandmother by now," Hayfa's daughter asked brightly.

Nalah smiled gratefully, taking her old place beneath the persimmon tree. "My daughter-in-law had twins, a boy and girl. They're grown now."

"That's so nice! Who did Youssef marry?"

"Youssef? Oh, no. They are Qaseem's children."

"Ah, quiet Qaseem with twins!" She paused, remembering something. "Didn't he work for the palace?" she asked in a low, concerned voice.

"Not for a long time now. He teaches at the International School."

"That is a relief. And what about Youssef? He was around so much for a while. Mama always thought he'd end up marrying one of us. I think she wished for it."

Nalah smiled sadly. "I would have liked that too."

Soon voices filled the hallway as the sisters and their families came home quarrelling and frantic. When they noticed Salim in the garden, they circled him, laughing and weeping. Nalah wanted to disappear. She was sorry that she'd made them worry. Once again her family was causing their pain. She watched as the sisters—now the age that she and Hayfa had been when their friendship was at its deepest—traced the scars on their brother's arms and then lifted his chin so they could look into his eyes. Briefly, the pain in her jaw subsided. When the room finally quieted, Salim sank onto the floor, exhausted. One of his sisters handed him a glass of tea. He cradled it in his hands for a second and then sipped it loudly. Amused, the baby crawled toward him and climbed into his lap.

Nalah thought of the other families she'd seen on the television and at the prison. When the joy and relief were gone, who would they blame for their lost time? Nalah had always blamed her husband. When he returned home from the police station on the evening of Salim's arrest and found Youssef asleep in his former room, the two men fought. Nalah stepped between them. One of their blows—she couldn't say whose—hit her jaw and sent her to the ground. Youssef left and never returned. With ice and time, the swelling and bruising went down, but the injury was permanent and the source of her pain today.

When Nalah finally left Salim and his sisters, it was dark outside. Her son and daughter-in-law would be worried. On the way home, she asked the cab driver to stop at a brightly lit shop that sold phone cards and money orders. Inside she pulled her husband's life savings out of her purse, requesting that it be wired to the account in Syria.

"All of it?" the man asked after he'd counted it twice.

She nodded, her jaw so tight, she could barely form the word. With the odd change she had left, she bought a cake for Qaseem's family, holding it primly in her lap as the driver rushed her home. A gift from Hayfa's family she would explain. "Careful of the sugars," she could already hear her granddaughter say.

NIGHT VISION

THE GUY was just standing there, killing time. These were the words Clark used to describe the first guy he shot in the war—to Tibbs and Lyons and the other soldiers, to the lieutenants and the cheek-biting captain with his chest full of brass pins, but never to Ned. To get back on track, he'd take a deep breath, sniff hard, and spit the thick phlegm near his boot. Killing time, that's how it all had started.

Clark and Lyons stood guard in the wide basement hallway they called the Dungeon, a place where weapons had been stored even in Hussein's day. In the pitch black, Clark couldn't see much of anything except for the blue glow of the light Tibbs kept on his key ring, which was dimming as he and Ned disappeared further down the hallway. They'd had a few beers, courtesy of a source that Ned refused to divulge, just as he'd refused to explain what it was he was looking for in the armory. It was a Tuesday, past curfew. This was one of the many stupid things the guys did to unwind and forget the gore of the day, one of the many things they did to kill time.

As Clark's eyes adjusted he was able to make out the neckless outline of Lyons who was rocking back and forth like a boxer in the ring just before the bell went off. Clark didn't like Lyons; the feeling was mutual. "You hear that?" Clark asked.

"Rats."

"I think one just ran across my boot."

"I've been trying to stomp on their tails," Lyons said.

"I can take about two more seconds of this."

"Copy that."

They stood in the dark a few more minutes until the armory door slammed shut and they could hear Ned punching in the alarm code. He and Tibbs hurried toward Clark and Lyons with four bulky contraptions in their uplifted hands: night vision goggles.

"Follow me, men," Ned said, and once again Clark found himself following Ned without asking questions.

They lived in a section of the abandoned palace inside the Green Zone. By military standards, they had it cush—walls and a roof, doors, showers, marble floors and a swimming pool, fans, barricades, even a unit of girls living above them. In the first seven weeks, Clark didn't see any serious action first hand. No car bombs exploding. No sniper fire whizzing by. No arrests. When he heard stories of unprotected outposts and soldiers going days without sleep, Clark felt guilt and a twinge of emasculation, but unlike the other guys, he never blamed the Army for not putting him where he belonged. Anyone who thought that what his squad did was easy should try it for a day.

Trained as an EMT, he was part of the cleanup crew, a unit that came in after an IED hit to rescue who they could and bag the rest. What he saw was secondhand—the aftermath, the victims, the families of victims. Consoling was as much a part of his job as tying tourniquets and assembling body parts for identification. His sergeant told him he had a serious case of empathy, not exactly a compliment, and used him as a liaison in the neighborhoods. Clark was the guy who kicked the soccer ball around with the kids, the guy who was sent to the morgue with a batch of fingerprints, the guy who delivered checks when the dead bodies were the Army's fault.

Most breaks, Clark sat in front of the oscillating fan in the make-shift rec room, listening to the other guys as they played cards or rounds of dirty I Never or Quarters using out-of-circulation fils, all of this accompanied by deafening renditions of heavy metal songs, too many cigarettes, and insults that more often than not leaned toward the homophobic or incestuous. Clark rarely joined in. He didn't smoke, he was terrible at telling jokes, he didn't hate Ali Baba. Lyons once accused Clark of thinking he was better than them, but Clark felt the opposite—that he was inexperienced, a terrible liar, and dull by comparison. He didn't even try to match the other soldiers' overblown accounts of what they would do if they ever got sent out on combat. The longer it had been for the soldiers, the tougher their talk. They spoke the same way about women, cars, and drugs. Ned was always the instigator of these conversations.

Clark hadn't liked Ned much at first. There was something sloppy and overdone about him, the way he said cheers, knocking knuckles over any little piece of news. Ned was thirty-three, the age of Christ as he liked to say, and as far back as Fort Lewis he'd acted like the ringleader, putting his hands on Clark's shoulders to let him know if he had questions about anything—from protocol to pussy, he was the authority.

From SoCal, Ned liked to sunbathe in his boxers in the little square of dirt outside their dorm. He brushed the leather toes of his desert boots every night, roasted marshmallows with his lighter, and ate Van de Kamp's clam chowder, mailed to him by his mother, cold from the can. Ned shaved twice a day with an electric razor that he kept in a zipper bag along with a canister of lip balm, a rubber-banded bundle of Q-tips, and a long strip of lubricated condoms.

Over time, he'd grown on Clark. His hedonism and self-promotion was an unattainable bravado Clark admired. As improbable as Ned's stories had to be, Clark found himself drawn in by the accounts of thirty-foot swells and weeklong drunken orgies. They reminded Clark of his uncle Frederick and the conversations he'd overheard as a boy. All talk. Occasionally through Ned's frantic eagerness, Clark could glimpse what he suspected was the real Ned: the Ned who Skyped his mother most Sundays, the Ned who was the first to include the new guy, the depressed guy, the ousted guy.

Late at night, after the others had fallen asleep, Ned would turn off his act briefly, admitting to Clark how much he missed "his girls" —his wife's long legs and the babysitter's cinnamon-flavored tongue, the way his oldest daughter, a first grader, stroked his eyebrows and his youngest, barely three years old, put her arms in the air saying, "Carry you." Then Ned might say something profound. "What is love, anyway?" he once mused, "but the desire to let someone know you."

In exchange, Clark told Ned about his uncle's bad heart and his mother coming out when he was young and how angry she was with him for going to war and how once, on a particularly maudlin night, he thought he'd lost her forever. Through all of this, Ned never judged. In the dark with Ned, Clark even dared to admit that he too was beginning to need more, to want things he knew he shouldn't— to witness firsthand how the messes they cleaned up got there, to see the enemy eye-to-eye—anything to drain the ache of adrenaline that had built up inside of him like a serious case of blue balls. With Ned, he found himself talking about anything and everyone, everyone except Sylvie.

Entering the hallway of the women's quarters, Clark could smell the difference immediately. It was the intoxicating scent of shopping malls and dozens of different deodorants, soaps, and lotions— floral and citrus, Jergens and Ivory—that suggested soft, smooth skin and reminded him of Sylvie. He thought of the way her clean, straight hair slipped from her ponytail. He thought of her skinny, childlike arms and the talcum powder she patted under those arms. For months he'd kept quiet about Sylvie, protecting her from this place and his horny bunkmates. Now, he discovered that the same femininity he'd simultaneously yearned for and shielded from the others had been here all along, just one flight of stairs above his own bed.

The four men left their boots in the stairwell, slipped on the goggles, and cautiously explored the central lounge area that funneled into a narrow hall containing three dorm rooms and a shower room. Tibbs whispered, "This is nice," and Ned nodded as if he already knew. Lyons lifted a stuffed frog, sniffed at it, and then tossed it back onto the chair. Clark felt wrong being there, yet what would happen if he left? Ned led them down the hall toward the room where Joelle slept. She was another of Ned's protégés, a plain girl from Lansing who more or less hated the other women and had been hanging out with Ned since before he and Clark became friends. Ned acted protective of Joelle although she didn't seem to need it.

They huddled just inside the bedroom door to get their bearings. Seen through the night vision goggles, the room was a murky green, as if submerged in lake water, reminding Clark of his mother's experimental films. A bunk bed lined each of the three walls forming a U with trunks and gear pressed between them. Tucked into each of the bunks, the women's warm bodies glowed like plastic figurines in a snow globe. Maria, a woman from a city near San Francisco made up mostly of graves, occupied the nearest bottom bunk. She slept on her side, her straight black hair strewn over her face, her arms and legs sprawled widely under her thin sheet. One of her feet dangled off the mattress. Clark had once heard her speaking on the phone in a language he'd never heard before, but when he'd stopped to listen, she'd turned her back to him. Now her delicate snore drew him deeper into the room.

Two electrical snaps in the old air-circulation system sent Tibbs and Lyons out the door. Clark held his breath, wishing he, too, were gone. Maria let out a deep, satisfied sigh. Using the wall to steady himself, he followed Ned to the bunk furthest from the door. There, on the bottom, slept Joelle. A stomach sleeper, her legs were pressed together, her knees slightly bent beneath her, pushing her ass into the air. Her face was turned outward on her pillow. She wore a wifebeater and a pair of workout shorts that said Spartans across the butt. Her sheets lay scrunched at her feet. Ned knelt down and peered into her sleeping face and then, like the father that he was, rearranged the sheets and carefully pulled them up over her shoulders. Clark watched, stunned. What if she opened her eyes?

Later, after returning the gear, the four of them sat around and shared the last beer, saying nothing. Clark remained lost in the mossy glow of the women's slow breathing and the floral-scented room. He kept hearing Maria's sigh, not from the safe distance where he'd been standing, but as if her mouth were pressed against his ear. Lyons wrecked the moment by pulling a tube of mascara from his pocket and announcing that he thought it was Claudia's. And then he pulled out Maria's tortoise-shell barrette and a postcard from Florida. Mementos, he called them, lining them up on the table like a museum display. The way he handled them proved to Clark that the guy was depraved.

That had been the first night, the magical night.

Over the next couple of weeks, the four of them returned to the women's dorm numerous times. Standing in the green haze, Clark felt as if he were entering their dreams. Each time, he hoped to recapture that surprised, aroused feeling he'd had the first night thinking of Maria's sigh, all the while worried that at any moment the spell would be broken. Every visit, Lyons took something with him: Maleeya's four-month-old *People* magazine, a jar of black nail polish, a key chain. During their visits, the women slept deeply and in the morning, simply accused each other. Then one night, Lyons had the audacity to snap a photograph of Maria.

A photograph was the sort of thing that got a person in trouble.

"It would serve you right if you got caught," Clark said to Lyons afterward.

"What are you, a mystic? Think I'm stealing their souls?"

"No, just stealing."

Clark looked to Ned for some backup.

Ned shrugged. "No one's making you go."

He was right. Clark had never said no, never hesitated or questioned out loud what they were doing, although he sometimes felt an acidic emptiness in his stomach that reminded him of the night of his uncle's bachelor party a few years ago. His father had complained about going, but there they were: father and son along with a half dozen middle-aged men huddled in a sleazy motel room on Division Street with a keg in the tub and a stripper who called herself Lana. The problem was that Clark knew her name was Lynn. He'd seen her community college identification clipped to the outside of her purse. After that, he'd had a hard time looking at her. What had been the invasion, he wondered now: seeing the plain name her parents had given her or how all of the men, including Clark, had started whooping it up when she pushed play on her boom box and asked, "Well, who's the lucky fella?" Clark had vowed then to never get himself in that position again.

Later, after the soldiers finally slipped into their beds, Clark whispered to Ned, "You know that person inside of you who you tell everything to—the one who is you, but not you?"

"Yeah?" Ned said.

"I think I've lost him."

Ned was quiet for a minute. Then he whispered tentatively, "Maybe I could be that person."

Without warning, the war got closer. One night when staffing was short, Clark's unit was given a search detail for insurgents in what was supposed to be an evacuated neighborhood in the south side of Baghdad. Clark and Ned were assigned a long rubble-strewn street and given a map, a two-way radio, and night vision goggles. The clear dark sky reminded Clark of the pre-dawn mornings during cross-country season when he pulled himself out of bed for a six-mile run. Once he was out, the frozen air filling his lungs, he felt in sync with everything—the tiny yellow light in the kitchen window of the Stanfords' house, the dachshund with the mangled foot who nipped at his ankles, the lone drivers who passed by with the lyrics of golden oldies spilling out of their rolled-down windows.

But this street had no lit windows. The pets had deserted. It was hot inside the bulletproofing. The only car was a single stripped-down chassis. The air held the pungent odor of burnt rubber. It was more of the same—the aftermath—made slightly more exotic by night vision. Clark and Ned quickly developed a rhythm as they secured each walled compound. Clark would take one side of the entrance and Ned the other. When necessary, they took turns kicking the doors open, the two of them shouting "United States Army" in unison.

Inside, the abandoned rooms felt surprisingly inviting. There might be pillows on the floor, a low table with an empty brass teapot sitting in the middle. In the kitchens, the white plastic chairs looked just like the ones in their backyards at home. The clocks on the kitchen walls kept the correct time. Clark and Ned were careful walking in—as if they didn't want to intrude. They walked into rooms where sky stood-in for roof. They walked into rooms with no fourth wall. In the distance, cats let out hungry yowls, but nothing glowed in the murk. While it felt to Clark as if he and Ned were the only two men in the world, somewhere behind these tumbling walls, the enemy was planning revenge.

The ninth or tenth house instantly felt different. Raking through the oven ash, they found an ember still glowing red. Out in the courtyard behind the structure, they could hear water running. A bag of pomegranate candies sat open on the table. Clark and Ned stiffened; it was difficult to read each other's eyes through the goggles. Clark gripped his assault rifle, preparing himself as he'd been taught. Knowing that something caught off guard was often more dangerous than something warned, he considered yelling out again, but then they heard what might have been a whimper or a stifled sneeze or a gun being cocked behind the draped door. Ned, whose turn it was to be the lead, was closest to the door. Clark waited for him to make a move, but Ned stood frozen. On the crotch of his fatigues, a circular glow expanded.

More frightened than before, Clark waved the nose of his gun at Ned, gesturing for him to move away from the door. Then Clark jumped through the door, pointing his gun in the general direction of where he'd heard the sound. His target: a woman sitting on a bed, stifling a squirming bundle tucked inside her black robe, a man holding the two of them, his eyes filled with fear and hatred. Through the crosshairs of the uplifted gun, the family was halved and quartered. The man on the bed spoke, "No, no. Do not shoot." Clark let his gun drop.

At that moment Ned stepped in. His rifle now drawn, he charged the family.

That night, in the yard behind the barracks, Clark and Ned lay on their backs, watching a distant refinery fire light up the sky with sudden bursts of red sparks.

"Like the Fourth of July," Ned said.

Clark didn't want to be alone, but he didn't want to talk either. He breathed in the cigar smoke from the rooftop where the officers and doctors enjoyed a nightly smoke. Someone let out a loud belch and they all laughed. Clark was thinking of the woman with the baby and the way Ned, ripe with the smell of his own piss, had approached them. When the man refused to stand, Ned lifted the blanket off the baby with the barrel of his gun and stared as it suckled loudly from the woman's breast and the woman struggled to cover herself. The husband offered up his hands for cuffs as his wife pleaded with him in Arabic and the baby began to cry. On the way to the military van, the guy spit on Ned's boot. In response, Ned shoved him to the ground. Clark tried to calm his wife. After they'd loaded the man into the back of the van, Ned held up his fist to butt knuckles, but Clark couldn't bring himself to return the gesture.

"Do you think they've released that guy yet?" Clark asked Ned now.

Clark could feel Ned studying him—his eyes going over his profile like Sylvie's finger tracing the furrow on his brow, the bridge of his nose. "We've got to get used to it."

"He wasn't one of them," Clark insisted.

"It's not our job to figure out if we've got the right guy."

"They looked so scared. Maybe someone had been there before us. What if Ali Baba was in the next room? We didn't even look. We just grabbed the first guy we found and got the hell out of there."

"What were they doing in there? Ask yourself that."

Hiding, Clark thought. He remembered his fear, the ridiculous leap he'd made through the door, and the target he'd made himself at that moment. "We both sort of choked out there, didn't we?" he said. "If it weren't for the goggles, they would have seen the same scared-shitless look in my eyes."

"Fuck you," Ned said quietly.

A few nights later, Ned convinced Clark to sneak back into the women's dorm, no Lyons or Tibbs this time, just the two of them. Clark hesitated, but he thought that Ned was on the verge of saying whatever he had to say to clear the air between them. More than once, he'd stopped Clark in the hallway when no one was around, grabbing his arm or shoulder in a way that said slow up. But every time, he'd shrugged and turned away. Clark looked forward to Ned finally admitting that he'd overreacted. He had kids and a wife. He knew firsthand how angry and helpless a father and husband would feel in that situation.

As usual, Ned led the way to the women's dorm. Once they were inside the sleeping quarters, he walked directly to Joelle's bunk. Clark stood at the foot of her bed, watching as Ned hovered over Joelle. Clark remembered that first night Ned had pulled up her covers. In the gesture, Clark could fully see Ned as the father he was—the father of daughters. Tonight, Joelle was sleeping on her back, her blanket pulled up. The room was cool and her face was a waxy glow through the goggles. Ned reached down and stroked her short hair. When Joelle opened her eyes, Ned put his hand over her mouth. She kicked a few times, looking from Ned to Clark, both of whom must have appeared frighteningly alien in their masks. Clark tapped Ned's shoulder and mouthed, "Abort mission."

Instead, Ned sat down on Joelle's mattress, his hand still over her mouth as he continued to stroke her short hair. Joelle did not fight back. Clark tugged at Ned's shoulder, but Ned shook his head. He wasn't going anywhere. Clark looked at Joelle, trying to figure out what she wanted him to do. The look on her face seemed to mirror his: not fear exactly but pleading, the desire to get the moment over with and, at the same time, the duty to protect Ned. Clark backed away and let himself out the door.

Safe in the stairwell, he pulled the goggles up onto the top of his head and tried to slow his heart rate, waiting for Ned. He held up his hand and watched it shake, swearing at himself. The longer he waited, the less sure he felt. What had he been a part of? What exactly was Ned trying to prove? Why was he willing to risk so much?

When it seemed clear that Ned was not coming, Clark went out to the courtyard for air. He settled into the lounge chair that Ned used for sunbathing to wait some more.

Clark woke disoriented. He must have been dreaming of Sylvie, because he was hard. He didn't think of her as often anymore—and certainly not in the old way. When they'd been together, he'd enjoyed the simple stuff—the hand holding, watching PG-rated movies in her parents' family room—almost as much as the groping that sometimes, but not always, followed. Then, just their bodies' rubbing against each other through denim and cotton was enough. Lately, though, his desire had grown explicit, ravenous. He imagined pulling her hair, biting her nipples. More. If before the soundtrack to his fantasies of her had been acoustic folk, now it was speedcore. As the other guys, including Ned, bragged about their girlfriends back home—the amazing head they gave, the skimpy panties they wore— Clark felt himself annoyed by the tentative way Sylvie touched his dick. From here she seemed exactly what she was, a sweet high school girl. Naïve, inexperienced. What the others would call a prick tease.

Sitting in the yard waiting for Ned, Clark pictured what it would be like to really fuck Sylvie, to slam his body into hers, to hear her sigh in that way Maria had sighed. He would push her onto her knees, pull her ass toward him, slide inside of her, hitting his hips against her buttocks again and again. What he pictured was something he'd spent months protecting her from. He gathered phlegm in his mouth and spat, and then pulled down the goggles to look at the puddle, the steam rising from it like a blue ghost.

Clark was brushing his teeth when Ned finally showed up at the sink next to him with his black case, not saying anything. His forehead was sweaty. His goggles hung down his back. It looked to Clark as if Ned had the beginnings of a black eye, a scratch on his upper lip. Maybe the women had ganged up on him. Maybe he'd hurt himself on the way out. Ned squeezed toothpaste onto his brush.

"Well?" Clark finally asked. "What happened in there?"

Ned was brushing tiny circles on his perfect teeth, watching Clark in the mirror. "You deserted me, coward."

"I thought you were right behind me."

"No you didn't."

"You were pushing it."

"Why is it you always side with the enemy?"

"The enemy? What do you mean by that?"

"You're always so worried about the Iraqis, but when we're cleaning up one of our guys, you hardly seem to care."

"I get it: that could be one of us. What's the point of saying it?"

"It's more than that. You don't get angry."

Clark looked into the mirror at Ned, who was accusing Clark of something serious: betrayal. "What's that got to do with Joelle?"

"Just that you don't seem to understand that you're one of us. A soldier."

"What are you saying?"

"If the girls are going to be here, don't you think they should contribute to the war effort?"

"They do."

"You know what I mean." With this, Ned thrust his hips.

"What the fuck did you do to her?" Clark demanded, pushing Ned hard against the wall and tightening the goggle straps against his neck.

"Go ahead, hit me, fuck me. I know that's what you've wanted to do since day one. Like mother, like son."

"Tell me you didn't," Clark pleaded.

"Didn't what?" Ned tugged at the strap, gasping for breath.

"Hurt Joelle."

"She wanted it."

Clark tightened the strap, insisting that Ned deny what he'd said until Lyons walked in and pulled Clark off Ned.

A few weeks after their fight, Clark and Ned headed down a narrow street that opened onto a small market plaza. Their friendship had cooled, but they were professional on their missions, a good team. Now when they patrolled, Ned insisted on being the lead every time. "Age before beauty," he said sarcastically as he opened doors with his gun. Whenever Clark saw Joelle, he avoided eye contact. He wanted more than anything to believe Ned—to believe that she had wanted it.

Patrolling that night, Clark had the feeling that they shouldn't be there. He'd come to understand that whatever hid in the dark should remain hidden: rats, packs of ravenous dogs, lovers wrestling in the barracks. He hated the false security provided by the night vision goggles. They made it too easy to confuse oneself—to forget that while the goggles revealed what was out there, they did not conceal the man wearing them. The counter intuitiveness of hiding in full view along with the required methodical, slow movements made Clark anxious, and the urge to run—not to desert, but rather to get out into the open, confess, be caught—constantly tugged at him.

There was someone up ahead. Clark gestured for Ned to stop. A man stood at the far end of the plaza, leaning on a crutch. He seemed to be alone, an ordinary guy breaking curfew to meet up with someone, a girlfriend maybe or a friend. The guy wasn't looking in Clark's direction, but Clark knew better than to pretend he wasn't there. All it would take to get his attention would be the accidental kick of a stone, a tickle in the throat. When the guy pulled a cigarette from his shirt pocket, Clark saw that the thing he was leaning on wasn't a crutch, but a rifle. Adrenaline surged through Clark's body. There was no safe way to find out if Ned saw him too. Clark carefully brought up his M16 and watched through the sites as the guy lit a match, simultaneously cupping the flame and checking the time on his watch in the meager light. Who was he waiting for? How long until they arrived?

How arrogant this stranger seemed, the way he leaned on his gun and inhaled deeply, just killing time. Clark placed his finger on the trigger. The fear, the unknowing, made it difficult for him to breathe. Or was it the hatred he felt at that moment—the natural urge to obliterate danger? He pulled the trigger and the guy dropped. Clark felt the same exhilaration he felt after crossing a finish line in a race.

He was turning to Ned when a second shot sounded. Clark dropped to the ground. Breathing hard, he flipped onto his back and looked up at the sky, taking a mental inventory of his body. An arm's length away, Ned lay on his back too. Clark poked him with the barrel of his gun and whispered, "You still with me?" Nothing. Clark shoved Ned with his foot and then slid toward him, whispering "Stop joking around, Fuckface." Ned's body was limp and sticky, but he was breathing.

Clark dragged him to cover and then lifted Ned's eyelids and felt his pulse. Once he'd radioed for help, he began CPR. As Clark pumped Ned's chest, he told him to hang on for his wife and daughters and girlfriend. He needed to love them enough to live through this.

Ned made no response. Clark pumped and pumped, silently begging Ned not to leave him alone out here in the dark. Ned's body released and Clark was overcome with the smell of shit, a mess someone else would have to clean up. Not far off, Clark heard what he thought must be the shooter running into the dark, his footsteps light as a child's.

BLESSED ENCOUNTERS

(AUGUST 16, 2006)
Dear Jamal, I am sitting on my bedroom floor, leaning against the wall that once separated us. Remember our Morse code knocks as children, the arguments we carried on after lights out? Did so, did not. I knock on your wall, but you are silent for once.

J, I can't sleep. The argument continues in my head. All of your life you made fun of Mum's love of Europe, her stories of growing up in London, her pride. How you resented English lessons. Now the two of you will have the language in common. I am deeply jealous. Although no one ever promised it to me, it is something I always imagined for myself.

The moment you boarded the airplane it felt as if my dreams had been yanked away. You, knowingly or unknowingly, are the thief.

You are afraid. I know that about you. I am sorry to say that this is the fact I hold on to in order not to hate you tonight.

Dearest Brother, Mum and Papa await your call to be sure you have made it there safely. In these two days, what have I done? Nothing, Brother, nothing of note. I start letters I will not send. I organize the books on our shelves. I memorize Snell's Anatomy, but for what? Who will ever test my knowledge? How many years will I study the human body without touching it?

Twin, we were always expected to share: space, attention, love. Even in the womb there was only so much room. Sometimes it seems my body remembers that time—the clasp of your legs, the nudge of your elbow, the warmth of your hover—but who knows. What I am certain of is your hands on my chalk, my books, my dolls—and the pleasure of letting go when you tugged too hard! We vied for our parents' love in much the same way.

I am beginning to understand that it was never a matter of measure—half for you, half for me. Rather, it was a matter of form. As the big-eyed girl, I received the cooing, the "clever girl," and you, the son, the expectation. How I yearned for someone to ask me to do something I could not.

I still see you walking away from us at the airport heading to my dreams. It was as if your leaving was the only choice. I have to ask, did you know how badly I wanted to go abroad? Had I kept the secret that well?

The lights flicker—and are out. Good night. Sleep well.

J, When I heard your voice over the telephone, I felt whole again and almost forgot how conflicted I've felt. I was too proud to ask: Do you miss me?

(August 26)
Dear Jamal, Morning brought the smell of burning petrol in the air, ash in the sky, and American helicopters buzzing our rooftop. The sound of the blades thrashing the air fills me with dread. It was much easier when you and I sat up awake through it all.

Up until now, we have been relatively safe behind our locked gate. The street violence is not as bad as last month; still, everyone debates whether or not this has turned from invasion to civil war. They say the last suicide killed thirty.

Dearest Jamal, Thank you for your letter! What a pleasure it was to unfold the pages filled with your perfect lettering describing that perfect place where you live. Mum was jealous of the number of pages, I could tell, and eager for me to reveal your secrets. I assured her there were none.

Now, how can I reciprocate? How many power outages or food shortages does it take to equal one scarlet-leafed tree in Michigan, the palatial study-rooms of Rackham, the university coffee shops where no one smokes? You say you are homesick. Let me assure you, there is nothing—nothing—worth missing here, except, of course, Mum, Papa, and me! Oh, and Aisha asks after you!

❀

(September 12)
Jamal, Baghdad has been quiet for almost a week now. I have had four full days of instruction. The ride to the university takes three times as long as it should. As you know, some streets are quiet and then, without warning, we enter a street in shreds, children sleeping on each other like cats, young men carrying machine guns instead

of book bags and briefcases, fewer women each day. The classes are nearly empty. Teachers do not always arrive even on the days classes are held.

The university has issued a memo insisting that female students dress according to conservative law. Aisha, Farrah, and I refuse. Mum supports me in this, but Papa is quite concerned. He says it is time to pick one's battles. I want to tell him that women are not given such choices. Of course, without classes our protest means nothing.

I began this letter in my notebook sitting on a bench during a break between Chemistry and Anatomy, but now the siren has gone off, one long blast to tell everyone to go inside. A car bomb somewhere, undoubtedly. Can it be that we Iraqis understand only the battlefield? Iraqi killing Iraqi. For what? We have fallen for the West's "divide and conquer." Al-Qaeda versus Hezbollah. Sunni versus Shiite. Sister versus Brother.

Papa does not like to hear his daughter speak so angrily, so I state it here.

(September 21)
Dear Brother, I have spent the morning with Mother sorting through Grandmother's old clothes. As I went through drawers of drab scarves reeking of her powdery perfume, I realized I never liked her, or she me. Sometimes I think she spent Grandfather's money in order to spite me. Surely, you knew she favored you, her prince. . . .

Ugh! Once again, this letter has gone in the wrong direction. I will have to fold it in half and toss it in the box I've started under my bed. Like my disappointments, the unmailed letters stack up.

Dear Jamal, It was nice to hear your voice, even if you were accusing me of avoiding you. I could use the excuse everyone here uses: no electricity.

We continue to "camp out." The sun heats our cardamom tea. We stink. Our generator makes a death rattle. How is it the Americans can deliver mobile telephones into our hands and no power into our homes?

Truth is: I write often, but nothing fit to put into the mail, nothing you would want to read.

J, Farrah spent the night. She is looking into transferring to a university in Cairo. Mum and I have had similar discussions. It is not my first dream, but I would welcome the change.

Jamal, Our generator finally gave out. A heavy heat sits in the house like an unwelcome guest.

Fifty dead in Sadr City.

(October 11)
Dear Jamal, Ramadan is coming to an end, and along with it, hunger during the day and eating in the dark at a silent table with Mum and Papa who are in the middle of one of their rows.

On the streets we are bracing ourselves against another resurgence. Police patrol our neighborhood supposedly in search of militias, frightening the Shiite families away. Remember the toppling of the statues, the waving of American flags? We wanted to be a part of the changes. We marched. We waved flags. We, too, had hope.

When our neighbors left, we thought they were cowards. We didn't want to miss our country's revolution. At times, I am not sure who or for what we are fighting anymore.

Dear Jamal, I dreamt of you. I opened the door to your bedroom and discovered that it had been blasted away so that all that was left were the jagged edges. I took a step, but there was no place for my foot to land.

(November 5)
Rapid gunfire in the air. Celebration. President Hussein has been sentenced to death. He rambles like a lunatic. Tell me, are the Americans rejoicing too? Be careful of falling bullets!

Dear Jamal, Papa has stopped speaking to Mum. I take that back. He speaks to her, but does not look into her face. It has been ages since I've heard either call the other *my love*. At night, I have seen Papa slip out into the garden to sleep; I no longer think it is in hopes of a breeze. The nights Mum works late offer relief. I wonder if you know what has happened between them. It's times like these that I miss you most. We could commiserate.

Jamal, You sounded different on the phone, impatient and a little agitated. First Mum and Papa and now you. What is going on? Are you OK?

(November 10)
Dear Brother, I have a job at a woman's hair salon! Everyone here thinks I'm crazy to have taken it, but school requires so little these days and I need something to occupy myself. I've been cutting our hair for years. It was the one thing Grandmother taught me—and then regretted when my precision with scissors led Mum to encourage me to look into surgery. I suppose if Grandmother were alive she would be the loudest protestor now! But, why not put the skill to purpose?

Papa has undoubtedly written, asking you to intervene. I'm keeping the job, so don't bother.

How many heads do I need to shear for an airline ticket to visit you? How many dark strands must fall to cover Cairo tuition fees? I begin tomorrow and have to admit that I am a little nervous.

(November 11)
Dear J, It went well! I found Grandmother's pointed scissors and took them with me for luck. My first customer was an old woman, Mrs. Hadal. As I cut, she barely spoke, her small black eyes following my every move in the mirror. Eventually I turned her chair away from our reflection so that she could not watch me so closely. When we were done, she hid all of my work in her shayla, left a platter of kleicha on the counter, and limped out the door. The owner says this was a good sign.

❀

(November 13)
Dear Jamal, Things are looking very bad here. Two more days of car bombings. Papa is refusing to let me attend classes. When I

mentioned work, he left the room in a huff. Mum drives to the mu-seum even when it is too dangerous. I suspect she does this to spite him. It's been weeks since I've seen the two of them in the same room together. Once when I tried to ask Mum what had happened, she took both of my cheeks in her hands and said only, "It is nothing worth concerning yourself."

Dear Jamal, I have a confession. It's been months since you left, yet I continue to have moments of self-pity and despair. I have so little to complain about in comparison with those who have lost loved ones. Still, in my darkest moods, I feel abandoned. No one fought for me, not even myself. I seek out people to blame. For months, I focused my anger at you. Now I watch our parents, trying to understand them. Papa is old-fashioned; I understand his decision—an obligation, really —to send the only son abroad and keep his daughter close. Mum always fought that sort of logic. She was the one to plant the seed: Leila will be a surgeon some day.

Today as I trimmed her hair, it hit me. Why, when the decision had to be made, did she desert me? I yearned to ask her. I was thinking just this when I accidently nipped the mole on the back of her neck!

Dear J, Papa and I met on Mutanabbi Street after our classes and walked the book markets, just him and me. I thought of you as we passed under the sign, READERS DO NOT STEAL; THIEVES DO NOT READ. I was tempted to ask him about Mum, but knew he would be evasive.

There are fewer and fewer children for him to teach each day. Still, he insists on going to the school for them. One of his children returned after a long absence with a bandage over his eye. Shrapnel wounds; he is blind in that eye for good.

Dear Jamal, Mrs. Hadal returned for a "trim." Her general attitude is one of perseverance. In this way, she reminds me of Grandmother. For such a quiet woman, she commands the room. She rings the bell to the salon and presents a plate of kleicha with a tiny bow. She is a frail woman with pointed features and a light moustache over her upper lip. She lives with her husband in what must be an expensive apartment that overlooks the Tigris. I offer tea; she refuses. She is glad to see me, I can tell, yet rarely speaks while I cut her hair. The salon owner says she comes daily, but only stays when I am here.

❀

(December 30)
Saddam Hussein has been hanged. Father was quiet all day. I heard him say to Mother: I have been betrayed. (His first real words to her in a month.)

❀

(January 10, 2007)
Dear Jamal, My first letter of the New Year and I am so sad. Saying goodbye to Farrah today brought back the despair I felt when you left. My paperwork is in for next term to join the Faculty of Nursing program at Cairo University. The three of us—Aisha, Farrah, and I —have been together since grammar school. Classes will feel strange without her.

Aisha is more distracted lately. She no longer speaks of transfer-ring. She will not admit it, but I think she is falling for her distant cousin. He's been away for five years, but acts as if he understands what we have gone through. I'm hoping her attraction to him is not simply inertia. It was not so long ago that she spoke only of you. As annoying as that could be, I wish for those days again.

(January 25)

Dearest Jamal, Remember the Assyrian Room in Mum's museum where we sometimes waited for her when we were younger? Remember running between the cases in the dreary closed gallery, dragging our fingers through the dust to collect static in order to surprise her with a shock?

I stood in that very room again today. I wish you could have seen it. No dust on the case tops today. With the help of the Italians, the dim salon has been transformed to a climate-controlled, video-monitored, motion-detected state-of-the-art gallery. It was spectacular. The walls were painted the color of warm sand to match the cloth decks of the vitrines so that the relics looked new. The jewelry was arranged to suggest a neck and head. Lit from inside, the alabaster bowls glowed. On the frieze, the nubs of the prince's beard had been polished clean. I saw why Mum had been working so many hours.

The museum is still closed to the public, but today, it was packed with journalists and cameramen, speaking dozens of languages. Mum fit right in, smiling and shaking hands, directing reporters to a case of recovered artifacts. Her English, which sometimes rose above the din of the crowd, was impeccable (at least to my ear). Seeing her in her element, I felt a twinge of shyness and the self-consciousness of being underdressed. Did she ever make you feel that way or is this particular to the mother-daughter relationship?

I'm not sure how to phrase this, but Mum made sense there. Watching her, I became even less sure that I would ever make sense anywhere. I started to cry in the middle of the crowd and turned to a case, pretending to study the exhibits as I gathered my composure. A young man I'd seen speaking with Mum asked me if I was OK.

I'm not sure why I'm here, we both said.

He explained that he'd come for help, but that he'd been sent away. Before I knew what was happening, I'd agreed to meet him tomorrow. I never did mention that the woman who had dismissed him was my mother. After he walked away, I noticed that in the case in front of us was the simplest linen fragment with the words BLESSED ENCOUNTERS stitched intricately along its edge in black thread.

Brother, Only a few hours have passed since I wrote. It's past curfew and Mum is still not home from the museum event. I hear Papa pacing. He is beside himself. At first he was angry. Now he is fearful. I can't sleep either. I wish you were on the other side of the wall.

Dear J, Both Mum and Papa (today they are in accordance about everything) have begged me not to tell you, but how can I not? Shouldn't you know how our lives are here? How ironic it is that we are trying to protect the one person safe from all of this.

Papa's worst fear came true: Mum was a victim of robbery last night on her way home. As far as I can gather, three young men climbed into her car and took everything—her purse, her jewelry, even the car. I cringe to imagine it.

The police brought her home around ten. She hasn't stopped crying. Papa holds her. It is difficult to recognize the woman I was jealous of just hours ago. None of us will leave the house today. If we had warm water I would insist that she soak in the tub with rose water. Of course, I will not meet the young man and he will be left wondering why. I know this should not bother me, but it does. Who can I blame?

(February 12)

Chlorine bombs. Now our people are washing each other away like terrible stains. Farrah says Cairo University bustles with displaced Arabs from so many places, it's as if she's in an airport.

Mum has given up driving! For now, Papa chauffeurs us around. They are finally speaking again. Papa is tender with her in ways I haven't seen in a long time. It is nice to have our parents back.

Dear J, As I placed the last letter onto the stack under my bed, I wondered for whom I was leaving them. Are they for you—or for me?

Dear Jamal, Finally, I have returned to classes. While stuck at home, I have committed to memory: the circulatory system, the skeleton, the lobes of the brain, and now the nervous system. As I close my eyes to test my memory, I hear you reciting the Leila sections of Al-Zahawi's poems to me. You and I are not as different as everyone has led us to believe. Aren't bodies and poems miraculous vessels?

Dear J, I cut the hair of five women in the course of three hours. My fingers ache. The impression of the scissor handle is set deep in my skin. My shoulders are tight from leaning forward so much. The women—and their hair—are a blur.

The ladies speak nonsense mostly, recounting scandals from *Forbidden Love* and then complaining and confiding about their own lives. When I don't pay close enough attention I lose track of whether they are speaking about themselves or the rich Turks in the soap opera. According to them, love, like tea, grows bitter or weakens over time.

Hearing them, I am simultaneously sad and relieved for never having fallen in love.

As they go on, I imagine the day I'll put scissors into skin, opening the human chest like the pages of my anatomy book. Can you imagine peeling back the layers of skin and fat and muscle, slipping your hands inside, and grasping a real human heart?

J, Detroit! Motown. I can't believe you went. Papa says it is one of the most dangerous cities in America. According to him, everyone has a gun and will rob you. After he said that I started to laugh. Finally he understood. I was thinking of home. Stay safe, Brother.

(February 20)
Dear Jamal, I had a surprise when I left the classroom today with Aisha. There he was—the young man I met at the museum!

We'd originally arranged to meet the day after the museum event, but then there was the incident with Mum, so I didn't go into Baghdad. Seeing him standing on the sidewalk clutching a tattered portfolio, I felt oddly renewed. I could explain myself to him. Something small had been returned to me.

For several hours, we walked along the sidewalks near the university, entering cafés and restaurants and bookstores to see if anyone would display his work. I know what you are thinking: imprudent.

A few shop owners encouraged him to unzip his portfolio and present his drawings—haunting black-and-white studies of faces and mythological creatures, some political in nature, others more poetic. Buraq flying over the downed statue of Saddam Hussein. A dove perched on a soldier's shoulder, its border asking simply: Where shall I land? Others were simply concrete poetry, except Rasheed (that is his name) has replaced the traditional verses with abstract words—blend, absolve, amnesia. The effect is unsettling. He is self-taught, but the calligraphy is almost as beautiful as Papa's. I know that you will doubt me.

The storekeepers looked through his drawings, one even bought a pen-and-ink portrait of the American president with his head wrapped in a keffiyeh, but none agreed to display them. We eventually stopped at a crowded café opposite the university. When we got to a table, he dropped the portfolio at his feet.

That museum woman was right, he said quietly. No one is buying art.

I didn't know what to say, especially since I have not yet explained that the museum woman who discouraged him is my mum. The more I know about him the harder it is for me to reveal who I am.

J, The authorities found Mum's car. She said she did not want it, but Papa retrieved it anyway.

(February 26)
Another meeting with Rasheed. After coffee, we made our way to a used bookstore. I walked beside him, admiring the weathered books and reading some of the titles out loud, worried that if I breathed in too deeply I would sneeze. I ran my finger along the bindings lined-up along the shelf, considering the English term, spine. And then, thinking of his intriguing face, his bones actually, I blurted out, how did you break your nose?

It's that obvious? he asked, laughing at me and covering his face with a book.

I'm sure the color in my cheeks told it all.

A car accident—when I was a boy, he explained.

I frowned.

It saved my life, he offered up, trying to relieve my embarrassment.

He told the most remarkable story—and one that didn't make me feel much better about my rude question. While he was in traction (a broken femur along with the nose), an American bomb blew up their store and the gas station across the street. His entire family died. Not knowing what to say, I finally asked if he missed them.

He smiled sadly—or maybe not sadly, but knowingly—and then said: Honestly, I don't remember much about them. At this point, it feels as if that life happened to another person. This is the life I know.

By then, we'd made our way to the art shelves with their hefty volumes. Rasheed stopped suddenly in the aisle. I waited to see which book he would pull from the shelf. Would it be Faeq Hassan or Jawad Saleem or a Westerner like Rembrandt or Francis Bacon?

Instead, he looked down the aisle in both directions and then leaned forward. I closed my eyes as if I knew what to do. When our lips touched it seemed as if I could feel the blood rushing simultaneously beneath our separate skins. It was the most frightening feeling in the world, one I hope to feel again.

Jamal, More sectarian fighting. I am stuck at home. No school. No work. No Rasheed. We've known each other such a short time, yet it feels as if he's been a part of my life forever. Still I have not told him my last name.

The Al-Asadi family next door has decided to move. Now only three families remain on our block. It is deserted and unsafe. I can tell that Papa is concerned, but doesn't want to further worry Mum and me.

The upside is that they gave us their generator—broken, but not beyond repair like ours. Papa and I have operated and now I can write to you under a dim light. After I fitted a new spring in the commutator, Papa looked up at me in the strangest way. It was as if he saw me—maybe even the surgeon in me—for the first time.

Thank you, Leila, he said.

I think he might have finally understood that I am not a child anymore. I am capable and can survive on my own.

Jamal, Sad and terrible news. Mutanabbi Street has been blown to ashes and dust . . . this is something I must tell you in person. I will miss my afternoons there with Papa.

(March 23)
Jamal, It's been over a week since Papa has allowed me to go to work and school. I miss the gossipy hens at the salon and Dr. Alousi's dull, incoherent lectures. I worry about Mrs. Hadal. I long for Rasheed. We talk on the phone daily.

It is strange to have something to look forward to. What is it that you look forward to, Jamal?

(March 30)
J, Finally! Today Mum and I will ride a cab into the city together. I will cut her hair as I always have. She says she is in the mood to shop. This strikes me as a good sign. It's been months since she's shown signs of caring about anything, even herself. I am glad to see her vanity return.

Dear Jamal, When Rasheed and I last spoke on the phone, he asked me if I would pose for him while he draws.

I plan to meet him at Shorjah market tomorrow where he works. I've told no one, not even Aisha. I can't imagine how it will feel to have his eyes on me for so long, especially after so much time has passed.

❁

Dear J, I need to tell someone about my latest encounter with Mrs. Hadal. I know I have mentioned her in previous letters, so hopefully you will remember. (Sorry about the sloppy penmanship . . . I am now in a cab to Rasheed for my first sitting, my travel expenses paid for by her.)

This afternoon it was just Mrs. Hadal and me in the salon. When she pressed a folded bill into my apron pocket, I refused. This, though, only made her more insistent. She removed her scarf. I wetted her hair with a spray bottle because, truth is, the woman has very little hair left. As I combed the strands carefully, I noticed a handprint wrapped around her throat. Greenish-blue, a bruise, two or three days old. It wasn't the first time I'd seen hints of abuse.

How is Mr. Hadal? I managed to ask.

Very distracted, I'm afraid. Her voice was raspy.

When I asked if there was anything I could do for her cold, she seemed perturbed.

You are studying medicine. Surely you must know I am not suffering from a cold, she scolded.

Not knowing what to say, I snipped a few ends and then started up the blow-dryer.

She sighed. I will survive, dear. I always do.

Are you sure about the tea? It might feel good on your throat, I tried again.

Mrs. Hadal addressed me in the mirror. When he sees me, he sees my younger self with my black crimped hair and bright lipstick. He is quite jealous. It's flattering, I suppose.

I appreciated her candor. When I spun her around in the chair so she could look at herself in the mirror, I tried to see what Mr. Hadal must see: her sharp features full and soft again, her thin gray hair thick and dark.

Was it love at first sight? I asked.

Mrs. Hadal grunted.

He is my second cousin. I did what was expected of me.

Did you grow to love him?

We had a good decade or two somewhere in the middle. I can't complain.

Before I knew what was happening, tears began to stream down my face and my nose started to snot up. She apologized for being so frank.

It's not you, I said. It was then that I realized: I am in love!

I confessed this to her on the spot, telling her everything that up until now I have confessed only to these pages. She listened sweetly. When I told her that I was going to meet him at the market stall where he works, she tried to dissuade me, but I would not give in. She looked at my bare head and grunted.

He is a good boy? A devout boy?

I nodded.

She pointed to my bare head. This will not do.

She removed the scarf from her head, the only thing hiding her husband's abuse, and told me to sit in the chair.

When Mrs. Hadal was done, I admired her work in the mirror. It was strange to see myself with a scarf pinned near my neck, my eyes and cheekbones so prominent, everything but my emotions hidden. We hugged, promising to see each other next week. And, that is how I went to see Rasheed.

✾

Dear Brother, I know everything I am doing is dangerous, but there are so few opportunities for Rasheed and me to meet. I study while he works. He draws, his eyes settling on me in a way that is difficult to describe. Sometimes he frowns and I straighten my back. I think of the Basmalas you and I practiced together so many years ago, the pleasure I used to get shaping the verses into flowers and pears.

How stern Papa could be when it came to the lettering of Arabic. Remember how tightly he squeezed your hand when demonstrating the proper way to hold the qalam? I watched closely, mimicking even the pained grimace on your face. Both of us felt the unfairness in it. You flinched at his harsh words; I yearned to be taken seriously.

My memory holds several versions of the tricks we played when Papa left the room. Was it you who started it, snatching my work from me, smiling triumphantly when he unwittingly praised it? Or did I offer you mine, smiling to myself at Papa's positive reviews? What does it matter now? The result was the same: I did not insist on receiving credit. You are now in the States and I am here. What I am trying to say is that I know I am as responsible as anyone for how things have turned out.

Dear J, You will be amused. I showed Papa a drawing that Rasheed gave me. It was the word *red* shaped into a pomegranate blossom. (It is one of a pair. The other is the word *red* in the shape of a grenade. For obvious reasons, I did not show this one to Papa.) Papa took the calligraphy, his forehead scrunched, asking me where I got it. I said a friend had drawn it. He handed it back with a nod. What he thought, I do not know. One of these days I will ask Rasheed to make something to mail to you.

(April 9)

Protests against the United States. The protestors are right, but what will happen if the Americans go? Farrah has offered to share her room in Cairo with me so I can leave sooner. Mum and Papa say there is no reason to keep studying in this dangerous, broken place.

I am torn. What sort of young woman am I? One who stays for love or leaves for her dreams? Oh no! I sound like a character from *Forbidden Love*!

Dear Jamal, So quickly my departure plans are complete. Meanwhile, I can't make myself tell Rasheed. I am a coward.

This morning I skipped class and snuck to Shorjah early enough to help Rasheed and his friends pitch their canvas awnings and set out their wares. Around the market there are posters of Muqtada al-Sadr and his martyred father. The call to prayer contained a call for jihad. Hearing it, I stopped unpacking and looked around. No one else seemed to notice.

The other day as my cab passed by a crowd of mourning families, I saw a father hold up the corpse of a baby girl white with construction dust. At that moment, I was once again ashamed of where I come from—privilege at the cost of others' lives. Rasheed never mentions our differences.

Across from his music stall, his friend Ali set out rows of sunglasses and several hand-held mirrors with cracked glass. Down a few stalls, another of his friends, Khalid, lined up his alarm clocks and bins of batteries. I helped him set a few clocks and wind them up. Rasheed traded Khalid a CD for batteries for his boom box. He put in some basta and the three young men, heirs to the canvas over their heads, danced together, their hands up high. For a moment, the call for jihad disappeared. I wondered: if we were to marry, would this be my life? I hear your doubt. I know you think I am being fanciful. So what? I make sense here.

I thought today I would have the courage to tell him about Egypt, but I was too happy.

Dear Jamal, The wall separating Adhamiyah goes up, protecting us from our Shia neighbors. Papa was angry to hear my thoughts against it, but he must see the danger of walls.

J, Mum and Papa are very annoyed at me. Twice in the past week I have been late home. When they call my mobile phone, I let it ring. It is strange after all these years a twin to be an only child with so many eyes on me. Remember when we used to compete for their attention?

J, When I placed the most recent ill-fated letter into the box under my bed, I was startled by how many have accumulated over the months. How I censor myself, the girl who never had a secret before. For so long, I had nothing to say; now I am overflowing with words.

Protests rise. In another life, I would join them. Today I secretly beg the activists to stay home. I fear violence will come and I will be unable to visit Rasheed.

(April 17)
Dear J, I finally told Rasheed that I was leaving. He assured me that it is for the best. I asked if he would consider coming too, but his aunt and cousin rely on him too much. To comfort me, he listed off all of the things he has already survived.

When I finally told him how soon my departure would be, we both wept. Before I go, he wants to transfer one of his small portraits of me onto a wall. Can you imagine—your sister's face spray painted on a public wall like a portrait of Saddam Hussein or Muqtada al-Sadr? You will hate the idea, but I am flattered.

We finally talked at length about my family. I tried several times to apologize to him for the disparity of our two lives. I could hear how absurd I sounded, yet it seemed so important for me to finally make my peace with it. Meanwhile, I owe you a letter postmarked Baghdad.

II

SHE'S YOUR MOTHER

SFO

CLARK GRIPPED the handrail and carefully stepped onto the down escalator. He was loaded on Percocet and one of his legs had fallen asleep. He saw her before she saw him: standing cross-armed in baggage claim, anxiously studying the empty conveyor belt. Behind her, two young men, their heads wrapped in keffiyeh, looked up at him and then disappeared into the crowd. Clark's heart raced. He was pretty sure they were not real. He took a deep breath and then let himself fall behind a wave of excited passengers, taking the opportunity to watch his mother at a hover. She wore a red corduroy jacket, a purple gauze scarf, and jeans rolled at the cuffs as if she'd been at the beach. Her gray hair spiraled around her tan face. She wasn't pretty, but presentable, a sturdy, capable-looking woman. Her car keys would be in her coat pocket, the exact change wrapped around the parking stub. From here, she appeared to be the kind of mother that he wanted—a mother who sent care packages and organized welcome home parties, a mother who had waited for her soldier son, breath held.

On the day he arrived home a month ago, there'd been no banner, no tearful hug. She'd stood hidden behind his father, looking nervous but not nervous enough. "Why is she here?" Clark remembered whispering from his wheelchair as his father greeted him. "Because she's your mother," he'd answered. When she finally reached out to Clark, her hands caught on the back of the wheelchair awkwardly, so that she embraced the chair instead of him. He didn't think he would ever forgive her for that.

As his escalator step touched ground, Clark wasn't sure what to expect. His bad knee, the awake one, had locked up, but he didn't want his mother to see that he still had a limp. Not yet. Above the baggage carousel, the reader board shuffled to his flight number. His mother peered through the crowd funneling toward her.

Clark swept his hand over the new growth on his military cut and stepped off the stairs. His mother stood on tiptoes and waved, making her way toward him. Over the years, they'd done exactly this dozens of times. He took a few steps, returning the smile and thinking against his better judgment that maybe this time it would work out. An electric burn shot up his leg from the meniscus to the base of his neck, waking all of the shrapnel wounds along the way. The surgeons had pulled out the shallow pieces (Clark had a vial full of the razor-like fragments of rusted car and ammo ranging in size from eraser bits to shark teeth), but the deeper pieces would take time to surface, possibly decades he'd heard. These writhed and hissed angrily under his skin like speaker feedback, growing into purple, puss-filled things—part burn, part puncture—that looked like Kaposi sarcoma, splinters on steroids, robot acne. Even with the meds, the attacks were too much. He stopped short, grimacing as he tried to catch his breath, grabbing onto a stranger's arm to steady himself. His mother's face washed with concern and then, with a blink, her smile returned. Whether she did it out of fear or shame or to relieve Clark of the embarrassment, he would never know. When she reached him, she wrapped him in one of her bear hugs that always lasted too long.

As he stood still in her embrace, willing the Percocet to lift him slightly from the moment, he could feel his mother's heart racing. She was out of breath. She wanted this to work out too. Overhead, a buzzer went off as the red light on the carousel flashed. Clark stiffened, fighting the urge to drop and take cover as the luggage carousel's conveyer belt jerked to a start and the other travelers shoved toward it.

"We're holding up traffic," his mother finally whispered.

When they'd moved out of the crowd, she took Clark's two cheeks in her hands. Her cold fingers were stacked with chunky silver rings. "You look good," she said, wiping his cheek. "You look recovered."

Two bald-faced lies in a row. Why couldn't she have done this last month when he'd needed it more? Clark looked toward the procession of black roller bags tied with colored ribbons plopping out of the chute. Finally, at the top of the ramp, the desert camouflage of his military duffle appeared, shooting way out before dropping. He pried his mother's hands from his cheek and limped deliberately toward it.

Fulton Street

THE FIRST thing Clark noticed when they double-parked in front of his mother's flat to unload was the sun-faded NO BLOOD FOR OIL poster taped up in the corner of her living room window. She'd had it up for years.

"Is that what you think I was fighting for?" he asked as they climbed the stairs. Next to it, but smaller and new as an afterthought, was another: BRING OUR TROOPS HOME.

"I thought about taking them down, but then I told myself that I needed to be honest with you, no censoring. Besides, they aren't directed at you, Clark, just the government and its policies. You shouldn't have had to go, that's all I'm trying to say."

"I wasn't drafted. I chose to go," he reminded her.

"I'm not judging your decision if that's what you think. I've made my peace."

They were crowded in the threshold of the narrow shotgun hallway. He looked down toward the kitchen. The place seemed empty. Theresa hadn't been at the airport with his mother like she usually was. "Theresa at work?" he asked.

His mother cleared her throat and looked out the front door window. "We're sort of separated."

Clark thought for a moment. "Divorced?"

"Regrouping. I meant to tell you earlier. Do you want some water, mint tea?"

"Caffeine, that's what I need." He knew that she didn't stock caffeinated drinks and he didn't need one, but he did need a moment alone.

"I guess I could run to the corner store."

"That would be great."

"Have a seat. I'll be right back."

He was already a little wired and it felt better to stand. Clark looked around the room. It was cluttered with flea market finds and stacks of floor pillows where there should have been chairs. His mother's movie camera was set up on its tripod near the unused fireplace. From the living room window, Clark watched his mother jaywalk toward Nimer's, a place he knew from past visits had Afghani television playing behind the counter. Since getting back, all of the news was about Afghanistan, as if the war had moved on. Clark couldn't imagine stepping into Nimer's now. Every time he saw skin of a certain shade, he was filled with dread. He knew that Arabs in general were not the enemy. But after being hit, his mind didn't always reason with his body. It had been trained to clench and go on guard for a number of things: sudden movement, sirens, human whistling, the flicker of a cigarette lighter. That, combined with a highly developed distrust of strangers, led to problems Stateside.

In Iraq, the feeling had come gradually. Early on it had surfaced as simple cultural annoyance when interactions with the locals did not go as planned. For these, he'd rebuffed himself, pushing the feeling inside and trying to see things from their side. Now, he no longer denied his deep-seated hatred. Blame was the only way to tolerate the pain in his legs and the fear that had overtaken him, yet the real assassins—the sniper who got Ned, the insurgent who set off the bomb that got Clark's legs—had walked free. When he pictured them, he saw them through night vision lenses, like phantoms in a bad dream: the guy lighting his cigarette on the quiet Baghdad street, the husband who had argued with Ned. These were the men who had thrust him into the war.

Outside, it was a typical foggy day. A guy with a seventies-cop moustache and polyester pants strolled by and then another guy, this one with cutoffs and a pink tuft of hair standing on his otherwise bald head like a Kewpie doll. It seemed to Clark that everyone who passed by was young and pleased with themselves, dressed as if they were indie rock stars or extras on a movie set. He wondered if they were all headed to the same freak show—or if in the time he'd been away, he'd become the freak. Did they even know there was a war going on? A couple pushed a double stroller down the sidewalk arguing over Thai or Burmese takeout.

Up the street a woman in a niqab approached, her eyes staring out at him through a gap in the black scarf. Clark backed up so she wouldn't be able to see him watching her. Whenever he went out, he was followed by Iraqis. They wandered along the roads and stepped out of elevators when he least expected it, but then disappeared. Sometimes they were women like this one, walking in pairs or pulling a child by the hand. Other times they were soldiers or kids in soccer jerseys and flip-flops. What did they want? None had ever done anything more than return his gaze. After she passed by, he stepped back to the window to see where she'd gone, but she wasn't there.

Just then, a hippie girl walking a dog looked up and gave him the peace sign as she passed. Two ordinary guys followed, each holding one side of a case of beer. Clark felt for the address in his jeans pocket. Before the officials came to take away Ned's belongings, Clark searched through his friend's things for contact information for his wife and girlfriend, finding nothing more personal than the return address from the most recent care package from his mother. The can of clam chowder and the surfing magazine hadn't been touched. Clark copied down the address and then hid the chowder in his own footlocker. He had something he needed to settle with Ned. As soon as his mother would agree, he planned to borrow her car and drive south.

He watched her cross the street, holding two plastic liters of soda by their necks. He carefully settled onto the futon. She filled a glass in the kitchen and brought it to him. She was telling him something about her most recent film—a "personal doc" using film she was painting by hand. Whenever she said doc, he thought of Dr. Paul with his green fatigues and the questions he asked, always referring to a scale of one to ten. How much do you hurt right now? How angry are you? What his mother meant was something like journalism, which in her mind meant truth. As she talked, Clark focused the best he could, but with the Percocet his mind needed something more concrete to latch onto. Outside, a semi idled at the stop sign causing the windows to tremble in their frames. She asked if he was hungry. Did he want a slice? A burrito? A burger? She listed the new restaurants nearby. Every mention of food made him queasier. He missed Theresa, the way she could diffuse his mother's nervous attention.

"Regrouping. What's that mean anyway?" he asked.

"Broken up, actually," his mother said, looking out the window behind him. She was sitting cross-legged on a large pillow with a blue Chinese dragon on it. She'd taken off her shoes. "I'm surprised she didn't tell you."

"What happened?" he asked.

"It was me; it always is. I fell out of love, same old story. Maybe I'm just destined to be alone."

Clark was silent.

"What about you and Sylvie? She must be glad to have you back."

"Why is it always out and in with love? Falling rather than walking or flying?" he asked, unwilling to let it go.

"I guess falling suggests a lack of control," his mother said.

"But, love is a verb, an action. Something a person has to do with intention."

"Oh, Clark, you know it's more complicated than just setting your mind to it. It's something you feel, something beyond sheer effort, don't you think?"

"All I'm saying is that love is something a person has to work at."

"Should love be work?" She raised her eyebrows.

Clark gave her an exaggerated shrug. "Should it be easy?"

She mimicked his shrug and then the room was quiet as he let her discomfort wash through the room. It served her right. "Sylvie is a lucky girl," she finally said.

Sylvie reminded Clark of something he couldn't have, except there she was, offering up every part of herself. Just tell me, I'll listen. Do you like this? Tell me what it's like. What about this? She would do anything for him and it bothered Clark that he didn't know what motivated her. Was it pity? True desire? Love? Every afternoon she showed up after school, her face and hair freshly made up as if the two of them were headed somewhere. They made small talk, pet the cat, watched television, and ate cookie dough that Sylvie made at home and brought over to bake fresh. Eventually, they ended up in bed.

Except Clark couldn't stand to be touched. The wounds hurt. Sylvie did her best to focus her caresses and kisses on his torso, which had been spared, helping him to forget the pain briefly until he'd guide her hands and mouth down to his shorts. She complied, never complaining, never asking what it was she was supposed to be getting out of it. It was all too easy. Afterward, it took all of Clark's self-control not to tell her to get out. He wondered now if his self-restraint was a form of love—or hate.

"You know, I could call Theresa and see if she wants to grab a bite with us. I'm sure she'd love to see you."

"That's OK," Clark said, shaking his head. He realized he didn't know how long his mother and Theresa had been apart: days, weeks, months? "I'm not feeling so well," Clark said. "The flight sort of wore me out." The Percocet had started to wear off and his legs felt twitchy and raw, making it difficult to sit still.

The next morning, Clark woke in his mother's arms.

It wasn't a dream. At some point, she'd slipped into his bed and wrapped herself around him. Clark tensed his muscles so that he wouldn't feel her as much as he got his bearings. When visiting in the past, he'd slept on an air mattress in his mother's cluttered editing studio. The mattress leaked so much that he often woke with his back touching the floor. But now with Theresa's office vacated, he had his own room and a double bed his mother had bought especially for him. The mattress was high, making it easy for him to get in and out. He assumed his father had told her what to get. He sat up and scooted away from her.

"Why do you do that? It's weird," he said, unable to hide his disgust. It had happened before—him waking to find his mother in his deflated bed as if they were two skydivers who had crashed down onto their chutes. He looked toward the window, trying to figure out what time it might be.

"When you were a baby, I used to crawl into your crib with you all the time. Sometimes it was the only way to make you sleep."

"You've told me that story."

"There was something so comforting about being caged in like that with you, seeing the world through your eyes. You were so perfect, so innocent. Lying there with you, I felt at peace, as if I didn't know anything other than what you knew—the dinosaur mobile, the cracks in the ceiling, the jiggle of the crib."

"Well, it's a little different now."

"I know."

"I've seen a lot more things."

She sat up and faced him. "Like what?" She was dressed in yoga pants and a man's V-neck undershirt, her eyes puffy.

"You don't want to know."

"Yes, I do."

"Death and dismemberment, OK?"

She closed her eyes. "Why do you have to say stuff like that? You never used to be so callous."

"You asked."

"How's your knee? What do the doctors say?"

"You'll be glad to know I'm not going back to Iraq."

"I'm not glad to hear that. I'm not glad about anything."

"The knee is fine."

"And the shrapnel?"

"Can we change the subject?"

"Show me your legs first," she said, reaching for the blanket.

He yanked it out of her hands and wrapped it close to him.

Tears welled up in her eyes. "I need to see what they did to you."

"This show is over. Get out," he shoved her to the edge.

"I know you don't understand this, but they're mine too. You're the only perfect thing I ever made—flawless. I can't stand the thought." She used her sleeve to wipe her eyes and then held out a closed fist and opened it. A pill bottle slid around on her palm. "Are these what I think they are?"

"Were you going through my stuff?" He thought of the letter he carried with him. Had his mother found that as well? It would be wrong for her to touch it.

"I thought the doctor said he was tapering you off of them."

"I still need them for the pain," Clark said, grabbing them from her.

"The pain?" She sounded surprised.

He collapsed onto the pillow and pulled the blanket over his shoulders, squeezing the pill bottle in his hand. He hated giving her the satisfaction of seeing how damaged he was. "If you cared so much, you should have written."

"I regret it. I really do, Clark."

"That's not enough."

"I know it's no excuse for not being in touch, but I truly believed that as long as I was angry with you, you would remain safe. As long as I looked the other way, danger wouldn't be able to find you. I felt as if I was hiding you from a jealous god. I never stopped worrying."

"He found me anyway, didn't he? Did you know that Theresa wrote me while I was there?"

"She told me."

"When guys asked, I told them she was my mother."

"I deserved that."

"But, I didn't."

She attempted to pull away his covers again. "Show me, goddamn it."

This time, Clark kicked back, pushing her off the bed with his feet as he struggled to remove the tamper-resistant cap from the pill bottle. When the lid finally came off, he poured three of the small blue pills into his palm. "Just bring me some water."

After the argument, Clark spent the rest of the day in bed, drifting in and out of sleep. In the quiet, he took out an envelope he'd brought back from Iraq. As afraid as he was whenever the Iraqis appeared, he searched their faces. The young woman who had given him the letter was never among them. She was different, real. More and more, she filled his thoughts. Even when Sylvie was with him in his dim room, he could close his eyes and there she would be, not a corpse or a ghost, but living and in his arms, her eyes still open, a trickle of blood pooling in her ear, yet never spilling. This was not at all how it had happened—their meeting in Shorjah market, his falling in love with her.

Undoubtedly someone was looking for her. Tracing the mirrored cursive of the Arabic, he apologized for making the letter yet another day late, once again attempting to justify his reasons why: the flight, the pain, the lack of sleep, his mother, the thing he needed to do with Ned. Truth was, he wasn't ready to let her go.

Barstow

CLARK LEFT his mother's on the fourth morning before she got up. When he'd broached the subject with her the day before, she'd acquiesced and given him her gas card and $200 for the road. She never mentioned his legs, the pain, or the pills again, but Clark felt watched. As he passed the living room on his way out, he noticed that the posters were gone from the windows. Her movie camera was perched on the mantel as if she'd been filming herself. Clark pushed the power button so that the battery would run out and stepped out the door.

Clark had been on the road most of the day when he pulled up to the address on the scrap of paper. Ned's parents' house was a small white cottage ruffled with bougainvillea and jasmine and tiny white roses. Walking up a wide ramp that led to the porch, what struck Clark was how much the place reminded him of his grandparents' home. He hadn't known them, but the house stood in front of his uncle's mobile home. Beside the ramp, a plastic milk crate was turned upside down, a makeshift step. Clark looked for clues of Ned's daughters—two bicycles leaning against the house, a dollhouse nestled into the grass—but there were no signs of small children, only a dusty surfboard resting next to the door, no doubt Ned's.

It was incredibly hot outside and Clark's mouth was dry, a side effect of the Percocet. He knocked on the screen door. A small dog started yapping. "Quiet down, Bobby," a voice said from inside. A small woman in a motorized wheelchair appeared behind the screen.

"Mrs. Sobrano?"

"If it's religion you're selling, I don't—,"

"I'm—was—a friend of Ned's."

She smiled tenderly and put her wheelchair into reverse to make room for the door to open. "I can see now you're military. What was your name again?" She was whispering.

"Clark. Clark Shepherd," he whispered back.

"I don't recall, but Ned had so many friends."

"I'm sorry to bother you," Clark said as he stepped into the dark house. A ceiling fan rattled overhead. A man snored on the couch; sports pages were strewn on the floor below him. The house smelled like dog. The wall over the television was filled with photographs of Ned from childhood: his tiny folded hands resting on a carpeted box, his grinning face wearing glasses, and then, years later, his hair dyed green and his glasses gone. His military photograph sat on the blaring television.

"He sleeps through just about everything, especially in this heat, and wakes up like clockwork for Oprah. Come into the kitchen. He doesn't like unexpected visitors."

"I'm sorry about—," Clark began before realizing that he didn't know how to finish. It was such a meaningless thing to say. For months one thought had repeated in his head: what if I hadn't fired at that sniper? But the truth was, he hadn't come to apologize. That wasn't enough. Since returning to the States, Clark had imagined this day, a chance to finally see the faces of the women he'd heard so much about, to finally tell them how much they'd buoyed Ned—and him—on those locked-down nights. Now, he felt as if he were intruding.

"I was there," he managed to say.

Mrs. Sobrano didn't say anything.

"It shouldn't have happened."

"We've made our peace. I see you're limping. Did that happen over there?" Mrs. Sobrano went to the refrigerator and filled a glass with ice and water from the panel in the door.

"Ned talked about you a lot," Clark heard himself say. Although Ned told lots of stories about this house and his parents, he'd never mentioned a wheelchair.

Mrs. Sobrano smiled. "He always loved his mother. That I can say about him."

"Ned was always taking the new guys under his wing, you know. He was a big brother sort."

When she smiled she had the same sharp points at the sides of her eyes as Ned. Clark went on. He told her about the morning that Ned had been shot. A few of them had spent the day at a hotel swimming and laying out by the pool. He thought that Mrs. Sobrano would be comforted to know he'd had a good last day. She kept looking over to the door leading back into the living room. "I don't want to be rude, son, but Daddy's going to wake. I'd rather he didn't find you here."

Embarrassed to have gone on, Clark shifted modes. "I'm here to get the address for Ned's wife." Mrs. Sobrano squinted at him. "There's something I want to tell her."

"Ned wasn't married." She smiled at him patiently, waiting for him to realize his mistake.

"Lucia, then, his girlfriend."

Mrs. Sobrano shook her head.

"But he talked about them all the time."

"You must have misunderstood. Or maybe you're thinking of somebody else?"

It was clear that Mrs. Sobrano had no idea who he was talking about. Clark couldn't understand why Ned would keep such beautiful secrets from his mother. Looking at the woman's hand on the knob of her wheelchair, he could almost see the red light in the hallway outside the room that he and Ned had shared, feel the wire coils in his narrow mattress, hear the sirens going off beyond the Green Zone. It was then that Ned would begin the stories about his girls. Mrs. Sobrano seemed sure that none of it existed. Clark's breath grew shallow and there was a tingling in his limbs that made him think he might faint. Before he could stop himself, he fell to his knees and put his head in Mrs. Sobrano's lap.

"Oh, sweetheart, we all loved him," the woman said under her breath, stroking his cheek. She rubbed her hands against his bristly hair. Clark closed his eyes. He could smell a faint scent of urine. It made him want to cry.

"Who the fuck are you?"

When Clark looked up, Ned's father stood above him, his T-shirt stained gray under the armpits. Bobby started yapping, jumping up on Clark's back. Applause sounded from the living room television. Clark struggled to his feet and held out his hand, "Clark Shepherd, sir."

"Don't 'sir' me. Every time you Army kids come around, you've got more lies to tell."

"Clark, here, was a friend of Ned's, Leo."

"A friend, huh? Then maybe he can clarify something for me."

"Sure," Clark said, standing. Ned's mother moved away from Clark so that he and Ned's father were left facing-off in the middle of the kitchen.

"My son wouldn't do anything disreputable would he?"

"Disreputable?"

"Some lady soldiers lodged a complaint."

Clark's face flushed. "More than one?"

"I never did think girls in the trenches was a good idea."

"What did they say?" Clark asked, following Ned's father to the door. "Was one of them Joelle?"

"They didn't give me their names. All I know is that no one can leave the dead alone. Kid, you need to get the fuck out of my house," he said, opening the screen wide.

Clark backed through, apologizing. He could still hear Ned's father as he got into his car. "See, Anita. What did I tell you? They're all cowards, covering their own asses. So much for loyalty." Clark slammed the car door and choked down a painkiller. What had he done? His hands shook as he turned the ignition; there was a frantic thump in his left temple. At the end of the driveway where the concrete turned to gravel, he pressed the gas pedal to the floor sending rocks behind him.

Big Sur

Unsure of what to do next, Clark headed back north toward Bakersfield. The endless reel of green and yellow crops and turnoffs to towns with banners for wine festivals and Renaissance faires made him anxious. Looking in the direction of these so-called towns, he located no settlements, no lights or rooftops breaking the monotonous flat. It was as if they'd all been obliterated. His hands were so sweaty that when he relaxed them, they slipped down the steering wheel. The surface wounds on his legs burned and twitched as if fire ants raced under his skin. On a scale of one to ten, this was a twelve.

Driving down, Clark had imagined finally hearing Lucia's deep-voiced Spanish and pressing Ned's wife, Kim, to him to feel her toughness dissolve into sobs. He'd wanted to hear the voices of Ned's girls. He'd wanted to give them solace, the way Ned's stories about them had once comforted him, to let their stories come to life and obliterate the loss. This hope had made it easier to ignore the occasional image of an Iraqi walking in the high grass along the shoulder between the outlet malls and freeway exits. Now, there were dozens at a time. He looked for the girl with the letter, knowing full well that he would never see her there. As he slowed to pass, cars sped past, honking. Clark turned off toward the coast, hoping to leave them behind.

He replayed the conversation with Ned's parents in his head, trying to unravel where the miscommunication might have begun, wondering if he should turn back. Ned, a man of large gestures, had always been full of contradictions. For the short time they'd been friends, Clark worked hard to keep order of it all. It was as difficult as fanning an entire deck of cards in one's hand. There were, after all, the wife and daughters, the girlfriend, the swells and bonfire fights, the broken rules, and then, finally, Joelle. "She wanted it," he'd claimed and Clark held him down ordering him to deny having touched her. There was no way to sort the lies from the truth.

On the tree-shaded road winding toward Big Sur, Clark began to feel himself relax. He pulled off the lid of the Percocet with his teeth and swallowed two more and then planted both hands on the wheel. His vision was a little blurry, but he felt more confident maneuvering the country highway than the straight-shot freeway. There were fewer cars and finally no Iraqis. The hammering in his head had dimmed to a manageable thud. By the time the road met the coastal highway the sun had started to set. Clark pulled over at a lookout and got out of the car to watch the orange disk slide down toward the black horizon. From here he could understand perfectly well why early cartographers believed the world was flat and the sun their very own.

A black Volvo pulled up beside him. A young girl begged to stay inside and a teen boy a few years younger than Clark announced that he had to piss. The father told everyone to shut up and let him enjoy some natural beauty in peace for once in his life. The man stepped out of the car, stretched, and then propped himself up on his front bumper. He opened the viewfinder on his video camera and aimed at the sunset. When the man wasn't paying attention, Clark stepped over the guardrail, following a faint footpath through the yellow grass toward the ledge. He settled there, folding his arms around his legs and resting his chin on his knees. It hurt to hold himself this way, he knew that, but the Percocet had raised his threshold of pain so that he was floating just above it, like the gulls above the water. It occurred to Clark that this was how most people experienced life—once removed like the man watching the sunset on the tiny screen of his video camera. This was how his mother experienced him, how he had experienced Ned.

He recalled an evening when the two of them had laid on their backs in the yard, their elbows touching. Overhead, a murmuration of starlings swooped back and forth into gauzy formations.

"Who do you miss most?" Clark asked.

"My youngest."

"Carry you," Clark repeated from an earlier story about the girl. "She's your favorite?"

"It's not that I love her more, it's just that she needs me the most right now. It's me she calls out for at night. Don't laugh, but sometimes when it's quiet, I think I hear her."

Over the Pacific, the sunlight thinned to a pink line. Dusk erased the land. It was a comforting abandonment. Clark realized that for all of his recent feelings of loneliness, he was rarely on his own these days. If it wasn't his dad or Sylvie or the PT or the Vet docs, then it was the Iraqis watching him. Overcome with exhaustion, he listened to the water lap against the jagged rocks below. The water was far, but the edge close. He considered that everyone was only a few short steps away from removing themselves from the past. All it took was a lie, a state line, a ledge. No one knew where Clark was at this particular moment. How good it would be to sleep in this very spot as an animal might, wake up in the morning, and drive in the opposite direction. It could be that simple to disappear.

Clark reached into his pocket and shook the prescription bottle. Empty. Until now, he hadn't realized how that small gesture had become a source of comfort for him. He reached his hand out as if to touch one of the birds silhouetted in the sky, letting the empty bottle drop. Rocks rolled down beneath him. He slid a few inches before his feet took hold. If he'd been standing, he would have easily tumbled over.

"Dude, you OK?" asked the teenager who must have been huddled just a few feet behind him. Carefully cupping a joint in one hand, he held out his other hand to Clark, pulling him up the steep bank.

Once they were a safe distance from the ledge, they leaned against the trunks of two wind-beaten sequoias and looked down toward the sound of the water hitting the rocks. In the last light, the birds were flittering specs, the crashing waves a distant *shshsh* as the ocean disappeared into the night.

"You scared me. I thought I was hallucinating," the kid said. He had long bangs that were combed down over his forehead. "Were you going to jump?"

"I don't think so."

He looked at Clark's shaggy grow-out. "You in the military?"

"Medical leave."

"You served?"

Clark nodded. "Baghdad."

"You look OK to me. What happened to you?"

"Shrapnel from an IED."

"Intense."

Intense. As if the war were a movie or a carnival ride or a video game a person could walk away from. The only people who understood where he'd been were dead or still there. There was nothing more he could say to these people—the ones who hadn't been there. That was the thing with war and the residual anger. Once you got home, there was no place to release it—no enemy zone or permission to shoot. Everyone here remained untouched, innocent. He supposed one of the reasons he'd gone to Iraq in the first place was to keep them that way.

"Was it scary over there?"

"It had its moments."

"You kill anybody?"

He looked at the kid with the joint in his hand and remembered the sniper lighting his cigarette. "It's not the killing that gets to you."

"What is it then?"

"The living."

The kid nodded as if he understood. The man at the car yelled down to his son. "Ready, Josh?"

He held out his joint to Clark. "Want this?"

"You sure?"

"Do me a favor and come up with me," the teenager told Clark, popping a piece of chewing gum into his mouth. "Don't say where you got it."

They climbed the narrow path at a safe distance from each other, reappearing at the cars. The father eyed Clark suspiciously, taking a deep breath. "You better not have shared any of that with him," he said.

"He didn't even ask," Clark said as the father and son got into the Volvo.

30 miles out of Santa Cruz

BACK IN his car, Clark rolled down the window and waited for the Volvo to pull away. He re-lit the joint the kid had given him and smoked it to his fingertips. By the time he stubbed it out, his nerves had settled. Driving north on the windy highway, he had to take the turns slowly and concentrate to avoid looking into the headlights of the oncoming cars. He felt warm, filled with a thick liquid, as if his torso were a lava lamp. Clouds floated inside his body. We all loved him, he heard Ned's mother say. Clark had never thought about it, but it was true. He had loved Ned. Only now it seemed that the Ned he'd loved did not exist. But the love—that had been real. If every liar needed a believer, then Clark had been Ned's. It was Clark's loneliness and need to believe that had enabled the two of them to inhabit the lie so fully. That had been their love.

He remembered the night that he and Ned fought—how each time he pulled the strap tighter against his friend's throat, he'd been trying to stop Ned from telling the truth about what he'd done to Joelle. Clark hit the steering wheel now. Could it be that the single time Ned had offered up the truth Clark had insisted on another lie? When Ned died, Clark had hoped that whatever had happened with Joelle had died with him. Now he understood: lies die; the truth lives on.

The sea air blew through the rolled-down window. The oncoming headlights sought him out like a search party. Clark felt the same urge to reach toward them as he'd felt at the sea cliff. He focused on the white line reeling him in and the glow he felt inside. A Foo Fighters song played on the radio: *wake up, you're dreaming.* He was getting close to somewhere.

Headlights appeared from around a bend as two clear circles. The closer they got, the more they blurred, spilling into his lane. And then a woman stepped out onto the highway and into his head-lights. She wore a blue apron with large pockets in the front, her dark hair tucked behind a scarf. It was her, the woman with the letter. Clark swerved, hitting gravel and then correcting himself. And then the car hit something hard and unmoving, the impact thrusting him forward. His head banged against the windshield. His ribs smacked the steering wheel. He imagined a mercurial liquid spilling out of him, filling the car with phosphorescent clouds.

Dominican Hospital, Santa Cruz

CLARK WOKE, flat in a dark room, asking for Percocet. The faint odors of antiseptic and burned coffee intermingled in the air. Some-one took hold of his hand and whispered that he should try not to move. He had no idea how long he'd been there. He closed his eyes and let himself drift off.

Consciousness came to him in waves. Sometimes he woke in the hospital or in his bunk or on his back in the middle of the street. Once for a magical moment, he'd been on the dock of Bear Lake in Sylvie's arms. When he woke again, the painkillers had worn off. His legs were icy and he realized his sweatpants had been removed. Only a thin sheet covered his legs. When he reached to pull it up, his breath went short. It felt as if he'd swallowed a knife whole. He remembered the darkness, the white line, the glow he'd felt inside, and a figure in the road. He let out a gasp.

At first, he believed that he was at the VA in Spokane, but as he gained more awareness he realized that the window was in the wrong place. The sound of the elevator outside was not a ding, but a buzz. The fake leather on the chairs beneath the mounted television looked to be blue, not beige. Later, someone was sitting in the chair.

"Clark, can you hear me? Are you awake?" his mother whispered, standing and stepping slowly toward him.

He almost shook his head no; the contradiction made him want to laugh which brought on another knife attack. It hurt so much that he couldn't feel the usual jabs in his legs. He had no desire to speak, to be present and accountable. His mother took his hand. "I got here as fast as I could," she said.

"The car," he managed to say. He couldn't bear to think of the person he'd hit. Was she alive? Was it her, the Iraqi woman he'd tried to save?

His mother put her finger over his lips. "It was used, worthless. I don't give a shit about that stupid thing; all I care about is you." She took his hand and squeezed. "You broke a rib."

"Where am I?" he asked, lifting his head slightly. If he was lucky this, too, was a dream. His throat burned.

"Santa Cruz," she said, pouring some water from a plastic pitcher on his bedside table and bringing the straw to his mouth. She brushed his hair off his forehead and looked into his eyes. "They found THC and high levels of oxy-something in your blood."

"I lost track, that's all."

"Clark, why are you doing this?"

He began to speak—as if there were an answer, as if he understood the question, as if he'd been aware of his actions. "Do you know how much we love you?" She put her hand on his forehead as if to measure a fever.

"We?"

"Me, your father."

"You called him?"

"Of course."

"What did he say?"

"He said he could be here if you needed him. I told him I'd ask you."

There was a brief bustle as two nurses came in, checked his chart, and then left.

"Did you see your friend's family?" she asked.

Clark nodded.

"It must have been hard on you."

He took a few breaths and looked up at the panels in the ceiling that hid the crisscross of water pipes and electric wires. He thought of Mrs. Sobrano, the one verifiable, good woman in all of Ned's lies. Her love was the one thing Ned hadn't been able to hide. Clark had hoped to comfort her. Instead, she'd been the one to comfort him.

"Would you have wanted one of my buddies to visit you if I had been killed?" he asked.

She thought for a minute and then shook her head. "To tell me you were a hero? Describe your last minutes? I'm afraid not. I would want your memory all to myself."

That was the thing about her love—it was greedy, isolating. Her answer seemed to disappoint her as much as it did him.

"What memories?" he asked without opening his eyes.

"Who knows for sure, but I guess I would think of that perfect day, the hours before you told me that you were going into the Army. I often think in those terms—how there was a time before and then a time after. Like the blue, blue morning before the airplanes hit the Twin Towers." Clark thought of the second before he fired at the sniper, when Ned had been alive. She was describing regret.

"Did I hit anyone?" Clark dared to ask.

His mother squinted at him curiously, taking his hand. "There were no other cars."

"Nobody in the road? No bodies?" Each breath pushed on his ribs as if weighted down by bricks.

"No one. It was just you," she said, smoothing his hair away from his forehead.

Clark remembered the Iraqi woman's eyes looking up at him through the rubble without fear or hesitation. Her eyes were the

same last night as he sped toward her, filled with the simple accep-
tance of the fact that she would die.

His mother continued to smooth his hair. "That day, I turned
and looked at you and you weren't my boy anymore. You were a man.
You had on shorts and sneakers and running socks and your legs were
perfect and lean."

"You're sorry I'm not him anymore, aren't you?"

"We don't need to talk about this right now."

"Just answer me," he whispered through the pain.

"Of course I am. Is it so wrong to wish you hadn't been hurt?"

He lifted his arm with the IV. "I need more."

She released the painkiller for him. As the liquid flowed into
his veins, he closed his eyes and listened to his mother scoot a chair
close to his bed and settle in. He waited to hear her shuffle through
her backpack, turn pages of a magazine, or pick up the television
remote control, but the room remained silent except for her breathing. Finally, he could make out a sniffle and then a muffled cry. He
realized then that she'd been staring at him all of this time, straining
to see his legs through the thin hospital sheet as if she were holding
an envelope to the light. He let out a sigh, his head sinking deeper
into the pillow, as his mother lowered the rail and squeezed herself
into his bed.

THE OPTIMIST

Qaseem woke in the garden with the same drowning panic he'd woken in for the past ninety-four mornings. He could no longer remember his own daughter's face. He gathered up his dew-dampened blanket and stiffly stepped into the quiet house. Sahar was still asleep in their daughter's room. He stopped at the chair where his briefcase sat. Inside was a manila envelope, lumpy with photographs of Leila he'd collected during the first few days, when he still harbored a reasonable amount of hope. The envelope was grimy from handling, the corners frayed. He pulled out the handful of photos, memorizing her again.

Like girls her age, Leila followed fashion. Her brows were plucked into thin arches, her eyes and lips outlined. She sometimes wrapped scarves around her neck, but rarely covered her head, especially for a photograph. She wore imported jeans and tennis shoes and thin gold bracelets. In each picture, her shoulder-length hair was arranged in various styles: a ponytail, pushed back with a headband, and his favorite, parted in the middle and tucked behind her pretty ears, making her look younger and less cosmopolitan than she was. He was surprised to see how much makeup his daughter wore, how much of her body she revealed, how unapologetic her grin appeared. He closed his eyes and attempted to conjure her beauty. Only when Leila emerged from the darkness of his memory could he open his eyes and begin the day. Would there be a time when he would close his eyes and she would not appear?

"Are you going already?" Sahar asked when Qaseem stepped back into the kitchen, showered and shaved. It was a rare hot water day, a reason to feel optimistic. Yet, a plate of day-old sweet rolls sat out on the table, a fly hovering. The tea, already cooling in their glasses, had not been double-brewed or sweetened. His wife slumped at the table, not yet dressed. These days she lived in a heavy housecoat no matter the weather or the hour. At times, the oniony smell of her perspiration was too much for him. Her hair, which had grown long in the past few months, was not brushed. Gray showed at the roots. Qaseem couldn't remember the last time she'd worn lipstick.

"You know I go out every day," he answered.

"And every day I'm here all alone. I go crazy in this empty house."

"It's my duty, dear. We've been through this."

"She's gone, Qaseem. It's been months."

"Have you seen a coroner's report? A body?"

Sahar flinched and looked into her tea. "I can feel it. Right here," she whispered, hitting her chest with her fist.

"I just don't understand why you choose death for her when there is no proof."

"A mother knows."

"And a father doesn't?" The question hung in the air. "Sometimes it seems that without me, she would be all but forgotten."

"You know I think of her every minute of every day." Sahar stood. "You want proof. You want a body. I wish you could leave her alone."

"How can I when we don't know anything?"

"What if I told you I saw her?"

"Why would you say such a thing, my love? I've been to all of the morgues. I've searched west and east. There is no body. I would know." Qaseem put his hand on her shoulders and looked into her eyes.

She looked away and stepped out of his grasp. She was crying. "This was the morgue on the other side of Shorjah."

"Why do you make up these stories? Don't you want her to live?" Sahar was quiet as Qaseem sat down and took a sip of his cold tea, his voice turning gentle again. "You will say anything to keep me home today."

"It wasn't supposed to be her," Sahar said, pushing her teacup off the table and leaving the room. The tea spilled, but the glass did not break.

Qaseem remained seated until he heard their bedroom door close. The roll and tea formed an unsavory paste in his mouth. He found a towel and cleaned up the spill, muttering to himself. What was the purpose of such a lie? Throughout their marriage, Sahar had mocked his optimism, equating it with naïveté and suggesting that he was a fool. She had no idea how difficult it was to maintain this level of belief, how much work it took to keep a shattered glass half full. What Sahar could never know was that he, too, wanted more than anything to stay home, to return to the garden and sit in the sun and never get up, to climb into bed and let Sahar—who had once been the strong one—curl her body around his like a vine. He wanted more than anything to give up, to let his daughter's face blur and then fade. But to do so would be to admit that what Sahar claimed was true: Leila was gone, dead. He had failed as a father. Qaseem picked up his briefcase, pulled a lightweight jacket from the closet, and sank down on the couch to buckle his sandals.

Sahar met him at the door. She wore one of her work suits. Her blouse had a stain by the top button. Her hair was pulled back and tucked under a flowered scarf. She held her purse in her hand. "I want to go with you," she said.

Qaseem placed his hand on the doorknob. "Not today," he said.

Tears welled up in her eyes for the second time that morning. She wrapped her arms around him. "Don't leave me alone with her today. She haunts me. I can't be alone with her."

Qaseem pried his wife's fingers from the back of his neck and kissed the tips. "Take a long warm bath while the power is on. Sit in the garden. It will do you good. You're pale, my love." He touched her cheek.

"Bring her home with you this time," she said without conviction, wrapping her arms around herself and rocking as if she were cold.

Qaseem rode to the city with Sahar's words in his head: it wasn't supposed to be her. What had she meant? Grief had made his wife indiscerni-ble. From the cab window, Baghdad had an abandoned, unrecoverable quality. The city had entered a brief calm, but the past year insurgents had moved from one neighborhood to another. Signs of the violence were everywhere. Monuments had been reduced to bent pipes, homes to rubble heaps, cars to burned frames, market awnings to shreds. Garbage floated on the Tigris. Soot stained every ledge. Men hid their faces inside balaclavas. Before Leila's disappearance, Qaseem had always, even after the invasion, been able to find something good in all of the decay—business owners attempting to rebuild, a mother smiling down at her child, old men playing chess outside of a café—small things that suggested the possibility of a return to normalcy. Now the scenes suggested only absence and pain, something to endure. It accused him of neglect. This was no place to allow a daughter to go alone. Yet he had.

The last time Qaseem saw Leila, she was getting into a taxi to go to the hair salon where she worked. He handed over her backpack as she climbed in, remarking on its weight. Leila laughed at him. "Oh, Papa. For an optimist, you worry too much." They were his daughter's last words to him. He knew she'd sung them out lightly, but could no longer remember them that way. Now, they were as heavy as the anatomy book that had most likely weighed down her backpack. Why she would have needed it, he couldn't say. He was sure she'd memorized the pages. Later that afternoon she'd called Sahar to say she was going to work late. In just a few days, she would be going to Egypt. But that night, she never came home, never answered her phone. The next morning, a complete void, a world without Leila. It was as if she'd fallen through a trap door.

In the first few days, Qaseem gathered together their dwindling savings in hopes of a ransom note. He visited morgues. He put up notices on the Internet. Leila's friend Aisha came along, the two of them approaching stranger after stranger, showing Leila's picture and saying her name over and over. Then he could still conjure his daughter's face at will and hear her voice in his head. Sahar believed that this was what he continued to do each day. In truth, he'd stopped the intense search weeks ago. Now he wandered the city most of the day directionless, the photographs never leaving his briefcase. Rarely did he speak his daughter's name.

When the cab entered the Green Zone, Qaseem got out. He walked toward the walled-off palace. He'd worked there once, showing his identification at the gate and spending his days in a small corner with his ink and poetry books, waiting for orders: a banner for a diplomatic dinner and verses to honor a martyr's anniversary. The gates were now guarded by young Americans in sunglasses with white paste on their noses. These uncomfortably large young men seemed unaware of the past, of tradition. Theirs, he speculated by their looks, was not a cultural pride, but a physical one. He'd once believed their presence would bring stability to the country. Now, he was no longer surprised when an American tank rolled by, crushing bicycles or cars along its path. Once he'd seen a parked bread cart flattened. When the vendor returned he chased after the tank, yelling and throwing crushed baqsam at it.

As always, the police station bustled with intention. Even after coming here for three months, Qaseem felt possibility the moment the doors closed behind him. Approaching the desk, Qaseem told himself that today would be the day a proper report would be stamped and filed that could lead him to Leila. He avoided the inspector, with his pirate's moustache. Since the collapse, the police were mostly Shia. He'd learned that it was best to present himself in a way that did not reveal his past privilege, but that first morning, when there was still hope, Qaseem had proudly handed the man Leila's photograph.

"She didn't come home last night," he explained, describing his daughter. "Tell me, have there been any problems near the medical university?"

"It's been quiet in the city since sunrise." The man smoothed his moustache for the umpteenth time and looked down at the photograph.

"And before then?" Qaseem asked, although he was afraid.

"Suicide bomb at Shorjah."

"My daughter would have no reason to be at the market," Qaseem remembered saying, his relief coming out as judgment.

"Then she is not among the dead," the officer replied.

Qaseem had not intended to offend the inspector. "How many were lost?"

"Eight have been found so far. Your daughter is the one who is lost."

"Their ages?"

"Three young men in their twenties, two old men in their eight-ies, a young woman," the inspector consulted the report, "probably the same age as your daughter, but it says here her family has been notified. The rest were children."

Qaseem gave himself a moment. Eight people, at least one of them a girl Leila's age. Not his daughter, but someone else's.

"Where could she be?" Qaseem had asked.

The inspector shrugged and then pushed the photograph of Leila back to Qaseem and said, "A young woman has no reason to be out in the city at night."

Qaseem took the photograph and slid it back into the envelope. He turned toward the door. "My daughter will be a nurse some day. I wish you the best of health."

With that, he'd walked away and back into the street to discover that the taxi driver he had paid to stay had not. It had taken him hours to get home. Now, standing in line for the young officer who always greeted him kindly and by name, his wife's words came back to him again. *It wasn't supposed to be her.* He wondered if he should ask the officer to look back to the day Leila went missing, but reassured himself with the inspector's words: a family had been notified. He focused ahead.

Behind the officer, a bulletin board was layered with wanted posters of Al-Qaeda and Mahdi Army rebels. Out of habit, Qaseem searched the faces for his brother. Like Leila, he'd left home one day and never returned, but that was decades ago. Qaseem couldn't be sure he would recognize his brother's face anymore. That was forgivable; time had passed. To forget his daughter's face was another matter.

Qaseem interrupted the young officer's greeting, "Sir, as you know, my daughter did not return home from work on April 26. It was a Wednesday. May I show you a photograph?"

"That's not necessary," the officer said, looking past Qaseem to where two men argued over a grapefruit.

Qaseem reached into his briefcase and took out the worn envelope anyway. The officer had seen the photographs of Leila dozens of times. Qaseem knew it was not easy to witness others' suffering, but he felt this was the officer's duty. Surely his daughter's life was more important than a piece of fruit. He carefully selected three photographs and unfolded the tissue paper he used to protect them. It was an odd thing to ask a stranger to look at a picture of one's daughter. It felt like a proposal. She was a beautiful girl, but the officer's eyes glossed over her images, registering nothing. He straightened the snapshots matter-of-factly, as if they were documents that needed to be filed, and then looked behind Qaseem again to the two men who continued to struggle. "Order or I will arrest you both," the officer threatened.

The officer's lack of focus struck Qaseem as more disrespectful than the inspector's straight-on, judgmental stare on the first night. Qaseem turned the photos in the officer's direction, encouraging him to look harder.

"Sir, do you have a daughter?" Qaseem ventured.

"No, I have two sons, praise Allah," the officer replied. "They are in Basra with my wife's family."

The man still had to look. Qaseem could not leave until he did.

"Please, take a look, sir. Think back."

The man relented and his eyes softened, giving Leila back some life. "I'm sorry, no. She does not fit any of the descriptions on today's reports."

"Of course not," Qaseem answered as he wrote his cell phone number on a piece of paper and handed it to the man. "Because she is alive. No need to apologize. This is good news."

He picked up each photograph, slid them into the manila envelope, and fastened it shut.

It was at precisely this moment each day that Qaseem felt his future become vast and empty. He had hours to fill before going home. He walked slowly to the door, blinking into the bright midday light as he turned and walked up the street. A few storefronts ahead, Qaseem came to a hair salon. Heavy curtains covered the windows, but because of the heat, the door was ajar. He stopped and looked in, staring at the dark hair on the ground until an old woman closed the door. At the corner grocery stand, the meager fruit in the bins was three and four times as much as what it should have been. Qaseem picked up a grapefruit and sniffed it. Did Leila like grapefruit? Qaseem couldn't remember. He wasn't sure if he'd ever known.

Qaseem strolled the relatively safe streets near the Green Zone before crossing over to the book vendors and cafés tucked under the balconies of Mutanabbi Street. In March, a car bomb exploded, destroying many of the stalls. One hundred people had been hurt. Around him, vendors had returned to business. The shelves and platforms were filled with shiny books in all languages as if nothing had happened, although there were fewer people browsing. He stopped at a display table and picked up a narrow volume by someone he'd once met at a party. Turning it over to read the description, he wondered how anyone could write in times like these. Somewhere in his desk drawers was a manuscript of poems, none of them relevant anymore. These days, the only writing he did was to his son Jamal in Michigan—long letters and emails encouraging him to study hard and avoid temptation.

A group of college students huddled nearby, flirting and laughing together. Qaseem watched for a moment and then turned away. For a few months up until the bombing, he and Leila had come here often, disappearing into their specific shops of interest—literature for him, science for her—and then emerging to return home together, debating current news and speculating about Jamal's new life. During these conversations, Qaseem was surprised to discover Leila's strong points of view, politics that often felt critical of his. It was this same sharpness of mind that had drawn him to Sahar, yet he'd never noticed it in Leila. For him, she'd always been a child—pudgy-cheeked, compliant, and in need of his approval. But those afternoons, he found himself seeking her approval and failing.

He knew why. For the first time as parents he and Sahar had had to choose. It was Leila who had spoken up, insisting that Jamal go to the States where he'd received a fellowship at the University of Michigan. Medical school, on the other hand, was a long, expensive endeavor even with the funding she'd been offered. It would be better for her to pursue nursing here. As she put it: she saw the country's need. Relieved, Sahar and Qaseem had let this be their answer. It was the same mistake, he'd realized too late, that he'd made over and over, in dinner conversations and in meetings with the twins' teachers. Qaseem was old-fashioned. He'd had ambitions only for his son and hadn't seen how capable Leila was.

He remembered when he'd introduced the Basmala to Jamal years ago. Leila was also at the table after pleading to join them. Jamal would rather have been on the soccer field or playing electronic games at his friends' houses. His work, sloppy and rushed, showed it. His palm had smudged the bottom half of the lettering. It seemed to mock the very god its words praised. Hoping to embarrass his son, Qaseem had switched the two, placing Leila's neat Basmala in front of Jamal and Jamal's rushed one in front of Leila. "Yes, that's it. Excellent work," Qaseem began, patting his son on the shoulder as he praised Leila's work, expecting Jamal or Leila to protest. Instead, Jamal smiled modestly, accepting the praise as his own.

Now Qaseem wondered about Leila. Had she heard the praise? Qaseem hoped so, but he didn't know because he hadn't bothered to look over. He and Jamal had been too happy in that moment, both of them finally fulfilling the other's needs. He had let Leila down in a profound way. During the afternoons walking with her, Qaseem began to suspect that she'd made the offer for Jamal to go to the States, not because it was something she didn't care about, but because it was easier to give away something dear than to have it taken away.

After writing a letter to his son in a café, Qaseem called Sahar to check in. He had no idea what she did all day. When he came home in the afternoons, he often found her dozing on Leila's bed, curled into a tiny ball. Qaseem always called in to her from the hall. To enter his daughter's room without her permission felt like a violation, another admission that she would not be returning. Yesterday, he'd found Sahar awake in Leila's room, so focused on a stack of neat pages in her lap that she didn't hear him approach. She handled the pages with the care she would a museum artifact. He suspected that it was Leila's journal, but couldn't make himself ask.

After over a dozen rings, she picked up. "Hello?" she asked groggily.

"My love," Qaseem said, relieved to hear the usual drowsiness in her voice.

"Oh, Qaseem. I was dreaming that Leila was still alive. Her voice was so close, it felt as if I could touch her. Please, come home. I'm sorry about this morning, but we need to talk. You have to listen to me."

"Just a few more hours," Qaseem answered, wanting more than anything to ask what his daughter's voice sounded like, how her skin felt.

"She was in love, Qaseem. Remember all of those times she was late? It was so unlike her. I should have known. Go to Shorjah."

Qaseem stood in front of the café, listening to his wife sob. In the spice shop window across the street, a pair of hands turned a sign from open to closed. Qaseem hung up before Sahar could say more.

It was past two o'clock in the afternoon when Qaseem boarded a bus toward Shorjah. He climbed the stairs to the top deck where Leila had preferred to ride even after she'd grown up. Out the window, a boy rode a bicycle through the puddle from a broken water main, creating a wake. Graffiti on the crumbling wall said: FAKE YOU, USA. The round face of Muqtada al-Sadr was plastered next to it. When the occupation began, he'd been barely a man, his beard thin and his voice weak over the crowd. Now the baby face ran Sadr City as if he were a modern day warlord.

The bus entered an area where fallen rubble spilled into the boulevard and slowed to a stop. The driver let out the impatient passengers. Qaseem took his briefcase and climbed down the stairs and followed the others out. The first few times he had recognized a human body among the debris, he'd averted his eyes, afraid of being ill in public, or worse, seeing something that would cause the victim shame. Now, he thought he owed it to the dead to look.

Qaseem could not imagine any reason for Leila to venture from her usual path. His wife's babbling made no sense, yet here he was with no idea where to go. He looked around for a sign that would direct him to a police station, a hospital, a district office, or the morgue as shoppers pushed him into the vast maze of the market.

Under striped umbrellas the merchants offered anything a person could need. He passed red tubs filled with lentils and nuts, piles of handheld fans and alarm clocks. Overhead, sneakers and dresses hung from rafters. It was loud with hawkers and music. People crisscrossed in front of him with white bags that read in English: THANK YOU FOR SHOPPING. He couldn't remember the last time he'd wanted anything.

He stepped into the daylight disoriented and unsure how long he'd been walking. He stopped near a pillar of wire birdcages to determine if the river was to his right or left. He walked away from it, turning onto a deserted street. He stepped over what looked to be the remnants of a restaurant: cracked plastic trays, a blackened teapot, opened tin cans, their attached lids reminding him of the mollusks that grew on the rocks along the Tigris. Muddy water seeped through his sandals. A turbaned man, skin sagging at his elbows, rushed past Qaseem and grabbed a dented kerosene can from a garbage heap.

A young woman walked toward him. She moved hastily and unencumbered. As she passed by, she caught his eye. Not knowing where to go next, Qaseem began to follow her. They entered a poor residential area that seemed to be deserted. After several turns, she entered a gate leading into a dim passageway siding a rundown dwelling. Qaseem hesitated and then entered the gate that she'd left slightly ajar. Roaches scurried along the cracked stucco. Techno music thumped behind one of the doors; laughter escaped another. In front of each door sat two pairs of shoes: a man's and a woman's. The woman stopped at an empty doorway and pulled a key from her sleeve. She was close enough that he could touch her.

"Leila, is that you?" he whispered as she unlocked the door.

"You can call me Leila," she answered, looking straight at him as she crossed the threshold. "But first, take off your shoes and set them outside."

Qaseem obeyed, but held back at the door. The walls were painted a deep red. There was a dimly lit bed in the corner, a table covered with a purple cloth. On top sat a pitcher and a stack of paper cups. He was desperately thirsty. A few times he'd been sure he'd recognized Leila in a young woman hitching up a backpack onto her shoulder with a certain jump, a familiar laugh, the same-shaped head bent over a book. He would stare or follow her for blocks, trying to glimpse the woman's face without frightening her. But this woman was different; she wasn't suspicious or afraid of Qaseem. She lit a stick of incense and sat down on the bed, removing her hood to reveal a small, pointed, heavily made-up face. A mottled pink scar stretched across one cheek and down her neck before disappearing into her abaya.

"What do you want?" he asked.

This made the woman smile. Outside he could hear a muezzin's call to afternoon prayer.

"That is for me to ask you. How much money do you have?" she asked.

As he reached for his pocket, she stood and unzipped her abaya, letting it fall to the floor, revealing the burn, which spread down her shoulder and the side of her body to her hip like a long continent.

"Please, put your clothes back on," he said, averting his eyes.

She reached down without hesitation, pulled up the abaya and zipped it closed, her expression never changing. "Better?" she asked, patting the bed as an invitation to Qaseem.

He was suddenly exhausted by the riddles. "Why did you lead me here?" he asked.

"You followed me."

Although it was true, Qaseem shook his head in denial.

"What are you, a police officer? One of Muqtada's men?" she asked.

"I'm a father," Qaseem answered.

"You're looking for your little girl, is that it?"

He nodded.

"Leila?"

He nodded again, tears welling up in his eyes at hearing his daughter's name.

"A lot of young women come through here. Most have no one, but if their brothers come looking I usually distract them from their search. You're different. I could tell when I saw you on the street. Do you have a picture of her?"

Qaseem pulled the envelope from his briefcase and watched as she dumped the photos onto the bed and pored over them, lining them up on the cheap satin sheet like a deck of American playing cards. She peered into each one. She picked up the photograph from the airport on the day Jamal left for the States. Side by side, the twins' similarities were easy to see. She smiled at them, leisurely studying them and asking where and when each had been taken. She picked up another, squinted at it, and then walked over to the tiny window for more light. It was the photograph of Leila with her hair parted in the middle, looking straight at the camera.

"I've seen her," she said, shaking her head with disbelief. "I'm sure it's her."

Qaseem grabbed the photograph from her hand and then scooped up the others and jammed them into the envelope. "It's not possible. Leila had no reason to be this far from home." He wanted to run, but the woman was unfazed by his slight.

"I'll take you. You can decide for yourself." She was already covering her head in order to leave.

He backed toward the door.

"Just come. What can it hurt?"

"Don't you understand? My daughter is dead," he heard himself say in a loud, emphatic voice.

Outside the brothel, worshippers with rolled carpets in their arms rushed toward the blue minaret of the neighborhood mosque. Qaseem joined them, hoping they would lead him toward a bus stop or a taxi so he could get away. Was he running from the prostitute or his own words? My daughter is dead. For months, he'd stopped himself from speaking such a thought out loud, even after the point long ago when he'd switched from searching for Leila to seeking answers for her disappearance. Along the sidewalk, vendors hawked faded photocopies of photographs of Muqtada and his martyred father. Qaseem stopped to let a man pushing a cart heaped with roof tiles cross. The young woman caught up to him.

"Follow me." Her eyes held the demand.

Qaseem said nothing, but let her get ahead of him a safe distance. As she walked through the crowd, men stared at her. Some said words that Qaseem could only guess. One raised his shoe. She led him to a bus station, but then turned up a street, looking down the narrow passageways as if seeking something. Finally, she stopped and once again waited for Qaseem to catch up. She took him around several corners where the streets were no longer crowded and the buildings were single story, their few windows boarded up. It looked as if a bomb had gone off nearby. A faded PHONE CARDS sign rested against a wall. One building was falling in on itself. A group of small children squatted at an open door, playing jacks on a piece of cardboard with the word UNICEF printed on it. The young woman stopped at a narrow alleyway between the two buildings and gestured for Qaseem to turn.

He had no idea what, or who, was waiting on the other side. Would it be a group of men with a gunnysack to throw over his head, police ready to entrap him with a prostitute? Certainly not his daughter, not Leila, not here. The young woman gave him a gentle nudge toward the alley. "She's up ahead."

Qaseem turned the corner, stumbled, and then righted himself. There, thirty feet in front of him, was Leila. Her black-rimmed eyes. The quizzical smile. The arch in her brows. Using the building for support, he approached her, staring at her face, now larger than life. He touched the cold brick: her cheek, her chin, her mouth. The mural, a black and white study with color only for the lips, filled the wall of this forgotten courtyard. Who could have understood so well the way the light molded her cheeks? Who had earned that smile? He saw then, words forming a calligraphic frame around her face. *Blessed encounters*, they read. He tried to remember where he'd seen something like it before. Qaseem turned to ask the young woman what she knew, but she was gone. He backed away to see his daughter more fully.

When his cell phone began to ring, he realized from the dim, pink light overhead that evening was coming. He'd been standing here for a while, memorizing his daughter's face. The phone rang again. A pigeon with a piece of shredded newspaper ducked under the eaves to build her nest. As the phone continued to ring, Leila peered at him from the shadows, impatient, reminding him of his duty, a father's duty. He pushed the button to answer.

"Qaseem?" Sahar called into the phone. "Where are you? Are you OK?"

He looked up at Leila's face smiling down at him benevolently. He was not OK. Leila was dead.

He'd said it once already today. He could say it again.

THE PACIFIC

"BUCKLE UP and bow," Walker yelled into the idling van's rearview mirror. Sylvie pulled her earbuds out of her ears and took her father's extended hand. Walker was the family name and what everyone, even Sylvie, called their father. And this was how the Walkers always prayed, their hands linked like circus elephants, trunk to tail: Walker to Sylvie, Sylvie to her brother Robbie, Robbie to their mother Claire, Claire to Walker. This is how they'd been around the dinner table three months ago when they received the phone call that Clark had been hit by an IED in Iraq. Since then, prayer hadn't seemed like such an assurance to Sylvie.

She tugged at her shirt to keep hidden the ugly bruise at the bottom of her ribs and then took Robbie's clammy hand, closing her eyes tight as Walker prayed. "Dear Heavenly Father," he began as Sylvie thought, please, help me figure out what to do about Clark. Sylvie and Claire amened in unison. Walker squeezed Sylvie's hand before opening his eyes and asking Claire to read some scripture.

Without saying a word, Claire lifted her white Bible from the mesh bag in her lap. Sylvie loved her mother's baptism Bible, white and soft as old-fashioned Easter gloves. She watched as her mother opened its gilt-edged pages to the New Testament, flipping through the red words of Jesus to Saul on the Damascus Road and the light that blinded him, causing him to change his name to Paul. It was a story about travel. Her mother's voice rose, "For I will shew him how great things he must suffer for my name's sake." Sylvie held her breath. The words made her feel guilty about Clark. It was as if her mother was telling her to stick it out.

She studied the light fuzz that glistened in the hollows of her mother's cheek where the sun hit. Lately Sylvie, who was not quite seventeen, had begun to study her mother for clues to the ways that she herself would change as she got older. Eventually, she wondered, would her hair turn that exact gray and her eyes sag and look sad in the same way? She hoped so. It made her mother look dreamy. Since going into full trip-planning mode her mother had become dreamier. Her voice trailed off before she finished her sentences and she asked the same question two or three times, claiming she hadn't heard their answers.

When the reading was done, Walker cleared his throat, looking once again into the rearview mirror at Sylvie and then Robbie. "Ready to hit the road? Rock 'n' roll, gang? California or bust!" Walker said. Religion time was over. Sylvie took a deep breath and pulled her shirt down over her stomach once more, telling herself that no one would notice if she would stop worrying about it for a while.

The Walkers were headed south through eastern Washington and then west along the Columbia River toward the Oregon coast where Sylvie would swim in the ocean for the first time. She wished Clark had agreed to come at least that far. The ocean water would have done his legs some good. From Oregon, the Walkers would drive down to the Golden Gate Bridge. In San Francisco, they'd visit Clark's mother, Jen, who was a filmmaker and had been a friend of Claire's years ago. Sylvie had overheard her mother say that Jen was going through a bad break up.

"I don't get it. Wasn't she a lesbian then?" Sylvie had asked her mother as they planned this leg of the trip.

"During Desert Storm, we waited for Walker and Clark's father together. Jen was there when you were born," her mother answered, her voice trailing off as she brushed the bangs out of Sylvie's eyes and explained that Jen's house was a bright-yellow Victorian. The word sounded pointed and velvety and filled with chandelier light. At the time, Sylvie had been excited to see Jen. Later, when she tried again to entice Clark to come along, he'd gone silent and then said his legs hurt and that he was looking forward to being alone.

As the Walkers drove south, Sylvie and Robbie played Slug Bug. With each Volkswagen, Robbie's slugs got closer to the sore place on Sylvie's gut. Her eyes watered. "Walker, Robbie's rough housing," she yelled up front.

"Stop whining," Walker yelled back.

"I've got a headache. Can't I just move to the back seat?" Sylvie pleaded.

Claire patted Walker's shoulder and nodded to Sylvie.

"Don't get too used to it, young lady," her father said into the rearview mirror. "I don't want this to turn into another one of those outings where you're off in la-la land, not part of the family."

Sylvie grabbed her book, a real pioneer girl's diary, and stepped over the seat to the next row. It was true. She often lived in her head and she could tell that it spooked her father to not know what she was thinking. She liked it back here, her feet pressed against the cooler, her head propped up on her pillow that smelled only of her. On the book cover the girl walked beside the covered wagon in a calico dress, her bonnet resting on her back like a hood. It was odd: the pioneers always walked west beside their covered wagons, but they never made it to the ocean. Sylvie wondered why they always gave up so early, settling for flat prairie land. She didn't want to be the same way.

She daydreamed about past walks with Clark. Last spring before he went to boot camp, they snuck to Bear Lake to hang out on the dock. Stirring the yellow skim of pollen on the water with a stick, he told her things she didn't know yet, things about Emerson and the Civil War and the railroad that he'd learned from his father, or about Magellan's slave who was the first person to sail around the world. He seemed to know everything. Before Clark left, she'd let him have it—all of it—and she hadn't been sorry. On the dock, they'd stripped down and spread out his cross-country sweatshirt so they wouldn't get splinters. It felt sweet and honest and as if she were finally telling him something he didn't know as he closed his eyes over her and the pilings squeaked against the planks. It felt as if they were in the hull of a boat arriving somewhere new.

Sylvie brought her book down over her face, breathing in the smell of the dry paper as tears soaked into the pages. Since his return, she'd wanted to be touched like that again, to touch Clark like that again without worrying that she would hurt him. They'd known each other forever, but he'd come back from Iraq a stranger. He didn't seem to be interested in anything anymore, not even her.

At the Dalles Dam they pulled over and stepped into the dry air to look at the view. Walker hiked up the road a bit and came back holding up a snakeskin on the end of a stick. It reminded Sylvie of the skin she peeled off her brother's sunburned back. Walker shook the stick teasingly at Sylvie, who pushed it away hard so that the skin fell on the ground at Robbie's feet.

"Pioneer ladies wouldn't be afraid of this old thing," Walker said.

"I'm not afraid of it. I just didn't like it in my face," Sylvie replied.

"Can I touch it?" Robbie asked, poking at it with his foot.

"Only if your sister does."

Walker was always taunting her, making her feel as if she were being a snob. She scooped up the snakeskin and cradled it in her hands. "See, I'm not afraid." She tossed it at Robbie and then walked to the ledge and took in the river rushing over the dam toward the ocean, wondering if this water would make it there before her.

The next day, they arrived at the fancy ocean-side hotel in Oregon where they would spend two nights. In the room, Sylvie opened the curtains wide. There it was, filling the lower half of the window: the Pacific, not at all the turquoise water and white sand that she'd expected. It was gray, the water breaking on jagged rocks. Luckily, their hotel had a pool. Walker, Claire, and Robbie put on their swimsuits, but Sylvie said she didn't want to change.

"Can't swim in your shorts, girl," Walker said.

"Don't torment your daughter," her mother whispered back.

"She's had her head in that book during the whole drive. She always wants to do the opposite of what we're doing."

"Yeah," Robbie said.

"Butt out," Sylvie told her brother.

Claire looked at Sylvie. "How about you put on your suit under your shorts. That way if you feel like getting wet you can."

Sylvie looked at her father and he nodded. Her mother always thought of a way everyone could win. Grabbing her sunglasses and notebook from her backpack, Sylvie hoped she could find the same sort of balance with Clark. Today she would write to him and let him know exactly how she felt.

Outside, it was hot and cloudless, the perfect day for a swim. The pool, blue and curved like a giant egg, was more like the ocean in Sylvie's mind. Several children floated inside bright donuts. A cute, tan boy practiced his dives in the deep end. The water looked good. Sylvie would have done just about anything to get into it, but she didn't want the bruise to show, her mother sighing, "Oh, dear, how did you manage to do that to yourself?"

Sylvie sat down on a lounge chair, situating it so she could see the diving board, and then began to write, sucking on the pen cap when the words wouldn't come. She didn't love Clark anymore. It wasn't his mangled legs or his twitchy body that she rejected, it was the darkness he'd brought back with him, and the way his gloomy, closed-off room that they rarely left smelled of sweat and dirty hair and antiseptic cream. They spent their time leafing through old magazines and watching obscure television shows on YouTube. It seemed to Sylvie that Clark was always cleaning his dad's rifle. Eventually, on good days, they would make out. That is until Sylvie would accidentally brush against one of the places on Clark's legs where the shrapnel was working its way up through his skin.

He was depressed; that's what the television psychologists would say. But Clark would tell the famous doctors to shut up before he blew their heads off. Sylvie knew this because she'd tried to give Clark similar advice. "This is what it feels like, all this lead," he'd said. The rifle wasn't loaded, but it scared her and hurt when he thrust the barrel into her stomach so hard that she fell. She should have walked out then and there, but she'd felt responsible somehow. The more she thought about it though, the more convinced she was that none of this was her fault.

By the time she was ready to flip over so she wouldn't burn, she'd figured out what to say.

> Dear Clark,
> Oregon has no sand. Its beach is pebbles and sharp rocks. I don't know how to say it, so I'm just saying it. I can't be with you anymore. I'd like us to go back to the way things were, but we can't. You need help. I hope you know I only want the best for both of us. Eventually, your feelings for me will fade like footsteps in the sand. Someday, you won't even remember who I am. You deserve someone better than me.
> With my sincerest ~~love~~ respect,
> Sylvie

It felt good to get the words out, as if her vacation could finally begin. She tore the paper loose from the notebook, and pushed up her sunglasses, half-tempted to join her family playing in the pool. Her mother, who hated chlorinated water and had gone in only to make it easier for Sylvie, held onto the white ledge to keep her head above the water. Robbie, who had on his mask, dove and kicked at the surface. A water drop fell onto Sylvie's page from above.

Walker was standing there, grinning. "Whatcha got there?" he asked. Sylvie quickly attempted to fold the letter, but he grabbed the piece of paper out of her hand, playfully. "A love letter? Are you pining for your soldier? No wonder you're so moody."

"Don't, please, Walker," Sylvie begged.

He stood above her with the sheet of paper dangling over her head. Sylvie jumped out of the chair, grabbing at it as Walker let it swoop low. Walker had been to a war, too, and her mother had waited patiently. He would never understand. She caught a corner and tugged hard and then watched as the letter sailed into the pool, where it landed on the water out of her reach.

"I hate you," she yelled. The pool area quieted as the cute boy stepped off the diving board and hugged his legs for a cannonball. Sylvie grabbed her notebook from the chair, slamming the gate behind her as the boy's body plunged into the water with a loud splash.

A few minutes later, Sylvie's mother stepped quietly into the hotel room. Sylvie was on the balcony looking out over the parking lot. "It's not what I expected, not at all," she said without turning around.

"What's that?"

"The ocean. It's rough. Clark told me that Pacific means peaceful."

"It'll get nicer as we go south, you'll see." She held out the wet letter to Sylvie. The words were smeared, but still legible in spots.

"Did he read it?"

"I got to it first."

Claire changed her clothes and the two of them put on their sneakers and took the steps down to the beach, bending to study the tide pools—the sea urchins with their purple spiked backs and starfish clinging to the rocks. Rubbery kelp waved in the water like the words floating off of Sylvie's letter. She wondered if her mother had read it and if she would say anything to her. Sylvie considered telling her the real reason she hadn't put on her swimsuit for the pool: how for two days after Clark got her in the abdomen, she had trouble moving easily, but now she was used to the bruise's tender tug. She'd tell her mother that's how it felt to be with Clark, too. There was always an edgy, unspoken pain under the surface of everything. It would feel good to get it off her chest.

Before she could speak, her mother put her hand on Sylvie's shoulder. "Your father doesn't mean anything by it. He's just an overgrown kid wanting all of us to have fun."

"He doesn't pick on Robbie the same way."

"He doesn't love Robbie the *same* way. You probably don't want to hear it, but you'll always be his little girl. Seeing how upset you are that Clark's not here makes him a little jealous."

"Jealous?"

"Once it was his job to protect you, make you laugh. He doesn't know what his role is anymore. You need to give him the benefit of the doubt."

Once again it seemed that her mother, in her indirect way, was telling her to give Clark more time. Sylvie scooped up a palm of cold water so she could taste the Pacific. More metallic than salty, she let it run out of her mouth.

After Oregon, it took them one more long day in the van to get to San Francisco. Beneath her T-shirt her bruise was beginning to yellow along the edges. There was a chance she would be able to wear the two-piece she'd begged for and get into the water soon. The Walkers' van rounded a bend and then the Golden Gate Bridge was there: a series of swooping red cables impossible to take in as a whole through the small windows. As they eased their way across the bridge, Robbie asked why it was red and not gold, but no one had an answer.

Jen opened the door wide and hugged each of them warmly as they stepped through the door, holding Sylvie in her cushy embrace longer than the others. After they brought in the luggage, Jen encouraged all of them to take off their shoes. Sylvie watched Walker give Claire a skeptical look and then kneel to yank his boot off his foot. Jen was the first to laugh at his big toe peering out of a hole, but she laughed in a way that made them all laugh. Sylvie couldn't understand why Clark hated his mother so much.

Sylvie picked up one of the many photographs of Clark from the living room mantel ready to identify the cross-country course and his place in the meet that day, but found she had a lump in her throat. Here was the Clark she loved, the one she didn't believe was ever coming back. She returned the photograph to its place and followed everyone down the shotgun hall to the kitchen, peeking into the extra rooms.

Jen's house was indeed castle-like, but she occupied only the lower floor. The rooms weren't grand, not in the way Sylvie had envisioned. The ceilings were high, but the paint was buckled and peeling in places and the furniture worn. It was dark and messy and filled with heavily patterned tapestries, old blue bottles, and rusty medical trinkets that gave Sylvie the creeps.

That night, she and Robbie slept on the floor of the dining room converted to what Jen called an editing suite. On a workbench, a reel of film was spooled into a viewer and then looped onto another reel with a crank. Next to it, long strips of film dangled over an old-fashioned drying rack. Earlier, when Walker slapped away Robbie's curious hand, Jen said the worst thing that could happen was she'd get an idea, maybe a good one this time. In a low voice, she told Claire that she'd been blocked ever since Clark's car accident. When Sylvie asked to see what she had looped into the viewer, Jen made a clucking sound and said there was nothing to see, just some old footage she hadn't used. Sylvie's face flushed as she remembered one of Clark's descriptions of his mother's films: pornos with fat ladies in them. Falling asleep that night under the filmstrips, she couldn't stop picturing plump cupids floating in the sky, sucking on each other's creamy legs and arms.

In the middle of the night, Sylvie woke to whispering in the kitchen. From the door, she could see Jen and her mother sitting in their pajamas sipping tea, their foreheads almost touching. Jen dunked her tea bag in and out of her cup. Her mother started to hum a John Lennon song. They both giggled. The clock over the stove read ten past two. Sylvie wished she had the same sort of friendship, but since his return, Clark had taken priority over everyone else.

When the two old friends began to stretch and say goodnight, Sylvie backed away from the door and stepped over her brother's sleeping body to Jen's workbench where she found a piece of paper and tried to write another letter to Clark. Rereading each line she felt sure that Clark would mock her. She wadded it up and hid it in the bottom of the wastebasket. What had seemed perfect in Oregon, now felt overly sure. Frustrated, she unwound one of the reels of film and held it under the desk light. There was nothing porno-graphic in what looked to be the smooth, green hill of a golf course. She scanned the frames. Gradually figures emerged over the hill, Clark among them. Sylvie realized it was footage of the State cross-country meet his junior year when he'd come in fifth. She pulled at the spool, trying to animate him again, to see his perfect stride as he crossed the finish line. How painless his exertion was then, his legs moving so smoothly they looked like spokes on a wheel. Sylvie imag-ined they haunted him. She thought she could understand his anger and was sorry for what she'd written, even if it was true.

Inside her sleeping bag that smelled of a hundred years of camp-fires, Sylvie slid her hands between her legs in the way that she al-ways found comforting and listened to her brother's snoring. She thought about what her mother had said about her father's love. She couldn't figure out what the men in her life wanted from her. Being near Jen, her dimples in the exact same places as Clark's, made Sylvie miss him, the old Clark with his racer's long stride who smelled of cold air after his cross-country meets, the soft-spoken one who could name all of the presidents on the bills and coins in her wallet, the hopeful one who'd read Emerson out loud to her on the dock.

The next day the four Walkers took a boat to Alcatraz, each of them following the voices of the audio tour through the long, cool rows of white cells where the Birdman and Al Capone had been incarcerated. Each room contained a metal bed frame, dry sink, and a narrow desk bolted to the wall where rust and concrete showed through the white paint. There were no windows, but the wind whistled and moaned through the building's cracks. Pigeons nested and cooed in the rafters above them.

The way the four of them gathered together like figurines in a diorama made Sylvie think of the times she dared to open her eyes during prayer to look at her family around the table. Robbie was fishing at something inside the sink with a scraggly wire. Walker stood in the center of the room, pressing his headphones against his ears as he looked up at the cracked ceiling. Claire stood beside Walker, their shoulders almost touching. She had her head bowed, her eyes closed. Sylvie wondered what Jen and her mother had talked about all night. Her mother folded her arms across her front as if she was cold and then started to rub the dry patches on her elbows. There hadn't been a quarrel or reprimand all day, not when Robbie dropped the sausage out of his McMuffin onto the floor, not when Sylvie begged to go back into Jen's house for the third time because she'd forgotten her camera. Walker hadn't even complained about the exorbitant price of the audio tours. Claire opened her eyes and caught Sylvie looking at her. She motioned her over and then pulled Sylvie into her as if she were trying to get warm.

When the audio tour was done, they kept wandering. Alone in another section of the prison, Walker rattled the bars in one of the rooms. When Sylvie's mother said he looked more like a monkey in a zoo than a criminal, they all laughed until Walker gave Claire a hurt look. Later, she yelled, "Help, get me out of here!" from the end of a long corridor, her voice bouncing off the high cement walls, but that time, no one laughed.

That night, Sylvie woke again. Not to voices, but to the feeling she was being watched. When she sat up and looked toward the door, Walker backed into the darkness. Sylvie slid out of her sleeping bag and padded into the kitchen after him. He was leaning over the sink, the water running. She turned on the overhead light, but he didn't turn around.

"What is it?" she asked.

"Couldn't sleep."

"Me either. Mom asleep?"

He shook his head. "Ladies' night out."

Her mother hadn't mentioned it. Sylvie wondered where they had gone so late. It made her feel sorry for her father. After a long silence, she asked him if he thought the place was haunted. No, just too much estrogen he responded. Half a joke, half an accusation.

"I think it's Clark," Sylvie said.

"Clark?"

"Haven't you noticed? There are pictures of him everywhere. But, no one's really said anything about him since we walked in the door. Not even his name. It's like he's dead." Sylvie wrapped her arms around her waist. In the light, she wondered if Walker would be able to see her bruise.

"Hasn't he told you about their falling out?" Walker asked, pulling out a chair at the table for Sylvie and offering her some tea.

"She left him and his father. I know, but that was a long time ago," Sylvie said, sitting down at the kitchen table.

"Not that." Walker filled the kettle and sparked the gas stove and then settled down across from her, looking up at the clock. It was the third time he'd checked it since she walked into the kitchen. "Jen doesn't believe in the war. When he was gone, she stopped talking to him completely—no letters, no care packages, nothing."

"Oh."

"I've never been fond of Jen myself, so maybe I'm not the one to say anything, but it seems cruel. I'd never do that to you or Robbie no matter what I believed."

"She came to Deer Park when he returned."

"A little late, don't you think?"

Sylvie nodded. She could see now why Clark closed up whenever she mentioned the trip, but why didn't he just tell her?

"Poor guy's been through a lot, but he's lucky to have you."

Sylvie wanted to deny it, instead she said, "Sometimes he scares me a little."

Walker focused his eyes on hers. "Clark's been through a lot, but time heals all wounds, you'll see. Look at your old pop: good as new." He patted his chest and crossed his eyes.

Sylvie gave him an obligatory smile. The kettle on the stove whistled and Sylvie jumped up to pour the water into two polka-dotted mugs.

"Having a fun time?" she asked, settling back into her chair.

"To tell you the truth, I'll be glad to move on. San Francisco isn't my sort of town. It's too crowded."

Her father picked up a photograph propped between the salt and pepper shakers. "Look at that," he said, handing it to Sylvie. It was a photograph of Jen and Claire sitting on a picnic blanket, bottles of beer in their hands. A young Clark was attempting to break loose of Jen's grasp; Sylvie, wrapped up in a flannel shirt, slept in Claire's arms. "That's my one regret—being stuck in the desert so soon after you were born."

"You're here now," Sylvie said, sliding the photograph toward him.

The two of them sat together at the table not saying much, blowing on their tea, and taking loud sips from their cups. After a while, her father looked at his watch and said he was going back to bed.

"She'll be home soon," Sylvie said.

He shrugged. "Sometimes a girl's got to do what a girl's got to do."

It was something he said when her mother went on a shopping binge or brought home takeout. He stood and kissed her forehead, wishing her sweet dreams.

Back in the room with Robbie, Sylvie listened for her mother's return, wondering what would have happened if she'd told her father the whole truth about Clark. Would he have become irate and confronted Clark or would he have sided with him, telling Sylvie that what Clark had done wasn't his fault? She wasn't sure she wanted to know.

Before long, Robbie's light snores lulled her to sleep. In the morning, Sylvie woke before everyone else and prepared a new letter for Clark, something more direct, less poetic than the first ones she'd written and never sent. She ended with, "I'm not a stupid girl. I won't put up with it," and then settled for a gentler way to sign off, "Love, Sylvie."

On their last day in San Francisco, Robbie and Walker went to the Exploratorium and the three women set out to walk to the beach. During the walk, Claire tugged at Jen's shirttail and smiled at the grimy street kids on Haight Street as if she was in on their secret. She dug into her purse and finished a peace sign arranged with pennies on the sidewalk.

Sylvie had never seen so many street people before. They were all ages and hung out together like misfit families. They even had dogs. The way they sat on the sidewalk at her feet, making it difficult to get close to the windows filled with sequined tops and sunglasses, annoyed her. Near the park entrance, a scruffy old man with an American flag pinned to the front of his hat approached them as they waited for the light. He was bouncy on his feet and smelled. Before Sylvie knew what he was doing, he'd grabbed her two hands. Looking straight at her, he said, "You, you know what I'm talking about," and then pushed her aside and stepped into oncoming traffic.

A green sedan slammed on its brakes and honked. Sylvie let out a squeal, but the guy just stood in the middle of the street waving to the cars.

"Why can't he get some help?" she asked her mother, shaken.

"Probably suffers from post-traumatic stress disorder," Claire explained.

"That and drug addiction. A lot of them camp out in the park where the cops can't find them," Jen added.

"What about their families?" Sylvie asked, looking across the street where the man was yelling to anyone who would listen. Neither Jen nor Claire answered. The man's look had been accusatory. He thought she was a traitor. If the mail was on time, Clark would be getting her letter today.

Slipping the envelope into a postbox the other morning, she'd thought of the care packages she'd mailed to him while he was away at the war: cheese and crackers and little bags of peanuts and shampoo samples. That was just months ago. In his early letters and emails, he told her stories of Iraq as she did her best to imagine the heat and dust and the women in their scarves. More than once, he helped Iraqi students bury their dead in rows of graves outside of Baghdad. Doing his best to rejoin the body parts, he matched fabric colors and shoes, and on top of each mound, placed an empty soda bottle. Inside of each, a rolled up piece of paper described where the body had been found, what clothes the dead had worn along with any identification the person might have held. In his letters, Clark described how sad it made him to watch the families walking the rows, reading these descriptions in search of loved ones. Once he found a letter in the apron pocket of an old woman who had died and mailed it off for her. Now when he spoke of Iraq, his voice was filled with anger, hate even, but never sorrow.

The three walked for a long time, past the rose garden, bison range, and then a windmill that had been shipped in parts as a gift to the city from an old queen. Sylvie admired its big weathered blades, unable to imagine putting something that large back together again. They crossed the busy street and were there, at the ocean. A pleasant surprise: the San Francisco beach was more beach-like than the Oregon coast. The sand was gray and crowded with towels and umbrellas and girls Sylvie's age with smooth, shiny tans and boys in long shorts that hung low off their narrow, unmarred hips.

Spreading out a Mexican blanket, Jen kept saying it was unseasonably hot. Sylvie wasn't impressed. Where they lived was hotter and this was California, it should be hotter still. Claire opened a thermos of lemonade and poured some for each of them. Sylvie watched Jen sit down and take off her sandals, letting her feet sink into the sand that was not white and gleaming, but dingy and scattered with bits of charcoal and kelp. The two women looked out at the ocean, not saying anything. Off on the horizon, surfers paddled toward a swell. Sylvie finally felt as if she'd made it all the way west. She pulled off her shorts and shirt and folded them beside her, sipping her lemonade, waiting for her mother to notice the undeniable grapefruit-sized bruise under her ribs. But her mother never looked in her direction, never said a word, except "ah" whenever the breeze hit.

After a while, Sylvie gingerly walked toward the water on the hot sand, glad when she could finally step into the cool tide that bubbled around her ankles. Slowly she stepped out further until she was knee-deep in the Pacific. Each time the tide swept back out, the sand pulled out from under her toes. A pop can hit her foot, rocking back and forth in the waves until it filled with water and sank. Sylvie imagined all of the bottles on the graves in Iraq floating out into the ocean, each one looking exactly the same, hoping to be found by the right person.

Sylvie started back. She wondered what Clark would do when he got his letter. Would he know before opening it what kind of news it brought? Would he hate her the way he did his mother? Across the highway, the windmill's wooden blades sat still. Sylvie wound her way through the patchwork of towels and coolers, stopping just short of the blanket where Jen and Claire lay close, their eyes closed. Jen sucked on the stone pendant on her necklace. Claire had a mosquito bite on her pale shin that she'd scratched until it bled. As Sylvie looked on, her mother bent her leg and stretched it, sliding her foot slowly down Jen's shin. The gesture, so intimate, caught Sylvie off guard. Jen smiled to herself and opened her eyes. Seeing Sylvie, she quickly moved her leg so that Claire's foot fell. It was a simple gesture, nothing much, but it was a correction, a suggestion that what Sylvie had just seen was private.

Sylvie backed away and then started to run toward the water. The sun was in her eyes. She thought she heard her mother calling after her. This only made her run faster so that the sand whipped the backs of her legs. We waited for Walker and Clark's father together, she remembered her mother telling her. Could it be that what she'd understood as common suffering was the opposite? Sylvie had no one to wait with, no one to tell what Clark had done. Up ahead, she could make out a father and son, a Frisbee wobbling in the sky between them like a flying saucer. The man jumped to catch the Frisbee and then released it back into the air. Sylvie ran toward it, widening her stride. She stumbled and then gained her balance just in time to see the purple disk fall into the boy's outstretched hands.

PEACHES

Bill woke before dawn on the morning following Ernesto Díaz's death. As he drove to the site, he tried to recall the wording of the memo he'd received last October instructing him to come up with a protocol to upgrade the BGF 100 timers at the crossings in his territory. Along with the memo, he'd received a case of ten replacements from Central Receiving—about a third of what he would have needed to do the job right. Centered on the top of the memo was the railway logo's acorn-shaped shield and below that the scant instructions that suggested something was not quite legit. At the time, Bill suspected the usual—a dispute with the manufacturer—and had left it at that. He knew the railroad was cheap, struggling, and perfectly happy to let go of a guy with any pension and the audacity to ask why.

Bill made the assignment into an exercise in statistics, spending several days tracking the intersections between eastern Washington and northern Idaho in order to decide which were worthy of the upgrade and whether to base his decision on the number of cars or trains that crossed or which were scheduled sooner for replacements. Finally he chose the nine crossroads that he knew were used by the local school buses. Unable to come up with a logical and fair way to identify the final crossing—the one closest to home, the one that was up next for replacement—he left the remaining device in its box on the storeroom shelf for an emergency.

It now bounced on the seat next to him as he turned off of the washboard road toward the intersection where Ernesto Díaz's truck had been struck nearly twenty-four hours before. This was the emergency Bill had inadvertently planned for, and it gave him a sick feeling in his gut. It was as if he had known even then. The words were most certainly not in the memo, but they were present now: failed, malfunction. There was no other reasonable way to explain a truck meeting a train as the crossing gate came down on either side of them. Bill had made the wrong decision all those months ago; now there was a wife without a husband and four children without a father. Love with nowhere to go. The railroad could easily find a way to blame the existing faulty timer on him. There were deputies making their reports, reporters snooping around, and a team flown in from headquarters. This was his way of letting them both off the hook.

The crossroads were still; the morning freighter not due for another hour or so. Bill pulled up to the side of the road just in front of where the arm and the electrical box attached to the thick metal pole and rolled down his window. It had been weeks since it rained and everything smelled parched, even this early in the morning when most would say it was still night. He turned off the truck, but left the key in the ignition so the headlights could shine on the box as he worked. Shattered glass glinted on the ground beyond the yellow caution tape.

The Díaz accident was gory, worse, Bill thought, than the helicopter crash he'd witnessed in the Gulf, but then he corrected himself. Not worse, but surprisingly the same, only more personal and devastating here at the lonely crossroads with its two sides of safety. On the other side of the tracks, Díaz's day would have been ordinary, just another crate-filled truck in the busy picking season. It was as if Ernesto Díaz was nearly home free, just ten yards to cross the tracks and eight miles after that to the warehouse where he would have unloaded the peaches which were still, like his body had been hours earlier, smashed along the rail.

This wasn't the first train accident Bill had seen. Now, he had to wonder if it had been the timer that had taken Leo Taylor's son, hit by a train on prom night three years back. That was on another track and before the memo. There had been talk that the boy had been drunk, so, in the end, the family had declined an investigation. Díaz was another story. With children and a wife left without a breadwinner, they would need money. Bill was pretty sure some lawyer would read about the accident in the Spokane newspaper, drive up with an offer to take on their case, and start asking questions.

As it should be, Bill told himself as he leaned over to feel around beneath the driver's seat for his flashlight. The space was oddly empty, the flashlight lodged back between the seat and the cab. Grasping the light, he realized his old Remington was missing from the seat coils where he'd kept it for the last ten years. He couldn't recall the last time he'd seen it. Maybe it had been missing for days, weeks, or months, even stolen. Maybe his son Clark had taken it out to clean. Could it be that Clark intended to act on his words?

On his way out of the house, Bill had found his son sitting in the living room, picking at the dark bruises on his legs. Bill stood silently in the hall watching him for a long time. On the muted television, buff actors rolled their bodies along the ground with the help of a blue contraption. On the table by the chair where Clark sat, there was an open beer can and a letter from his girlfriend, Sylvie, that he'd received the day before. Since she'd left for vacation with her family, Clark hadn't really moved from that chair. The living room was beginning to smell like a sick room. Bill would have liked to ask what the letter said, if Sylvie was having a nice time in California, but his son was picking anxiously at a blister on his shin.

Bill hated thinking of the shrapnel inside his son, the way they'd taken possession of not only his legs, but his psyche. Even as one sore healed, another always seemed to pop up. Now that he was off

Percocet, Clark obsessively picked at the scabs. This morning in the dark, he swore to himself as he scratched, "I wish I'd lost them. Better yet, I wish I'd lost my whole self—my legs, my brain. I wish I were dead."

Bill stood quietly, contemplating what to do next. Had the words been intended for him? Talk felt flimsy around Clark; half the time Bill didn't bother to say anything even when he knew he should. Now at the crossroads, he tried to remember if the Remington had been somewhere in the shadows of that dimly lit room. He couldn't see it there—but he couldn't be entirely sure. Fighting the strong urge to rush back to his son, Bill opened the truck door and stepped down from the cab. As his open door chimed into the early morning quiet, he walked purposefully to the crossing gate.

A helium balloon with a teddy bear was tied to the pole and a bouquet of daisies leaned against the base. He had to push the balloon out of his way to get to the electrical box. The metal door creaked on its hinge as he unlocked and opened it. He shined his flashlight in at the maintenance record taped inside. The timer was three years old. Sure enough, it was the BGF 100. According to the log, Bill had been the one to put it in. He pulled the sheet off the door and crumpled it into his pocket. Unwiring the old timer, he held it in his hand. Here it was: the thing that had made all of the difference, no bigger than a heart or one of the peaches on the ground. No heavier than a shoe. The matter of seconds: a hammer, a spring, turning gears. It was this sort of timing that had placed Clark far enough from a suicide bomb to allow him his life; it was this sort of timing that had filled his son's legs with metal.

Bill believed life was about timing, that each day had its own series of crossings. Sometimes a person would have to wait at them, staring out as the empty boxcars passed by—like the summer Jen said she was unhappy and was choosing between him and her "real self" or the months when Clark was away at war. Other times, there would be nothing to hold a person back. Good timing. He thought of Clark on the cross-country course, his slim, muscular legs moving evenly as he broke from a pack of runners. It wasn't something a person could control entirely. Bill remembered waving to his brother-in-law Frederick for the last time at the crossroads up the highway. When the arms lifted and the two passed by each other, Frederick held up an imaginary beer to his mouth to suggest they meet later for a drink. A few hours later, he was dead from a heart attack on the side of the road.

Bill took the new timer out of the box and plastic pouch. It was clean and almost shimmered next to the other rusty parts. He let it drop to the ground so that it would more quickly build up a dusty patina and look as if it had been there a while. He clicked it into place and attached the wires to the screws. If they started to ask questions, he would simply revert to the truth. He'd changed it after the accident, following protocol. By then, the faulty timer would be deep in the landfill and its history gone. No one would ever know if he'd changed it those months ago or not.

Bill pushed the test button and backed away from the pole to watch as the lights on the crossing barrier began to flash and the arm slowly lowered. He picked up the clump of daisies and sniffed, then locked the box. He was moving slowly, and he knew this was wrong. He should be hurrying to get back to tell his son that it wasn't up to him to decide the timing of his life. He had survived for a reason.

After the accident, Marisela Díaz arrived with her four children, calm and dignified. The deputies tried to keep her from the tracks, but when she caught sight of her husband's mangled pickup behind the fire truck, she broke away and ran up to look in its shattered window. She slid down onto the gravel and broken glass. No one knew how to comfort her. When the children saw their mother crying, they began to wail too.

The intersection was cleared now, as if nothing had happened. That was how the railroad company liked it. The coroner's office had taken away the body. The deputies had gathered what was left of the dead man's possessions and put them into an empty peach crate—a loose shoe, his shattered and bent sunglasses and watch, the felt cross that hung from the rearview mirror. Then, the cleanup crew had moved in to do the best they could with the metal and glass. Even the derailed train had been dragged away. Was this the finality his son wanted? It made Bill sad to think he understood.

Bill walked toward the rail, stepping on a peach and then another. Balancing on a tie, he tried to see what Ernesto had seen. The tracks curved out from behind a patch of cattails. Ernesto had never seen the oncoming train, at least not until it was right there on him. Maybe Bill should wait and make sure the train triggered the timer correctly; maybe he should be getting back to his son.

The sky was turning pink and the flies starting to buzz. Bill reached into his pocket and pulled out his pocketknife to cut the string to the balloon, watching as it lifted up over the pole. "I'm protecting us," he said out loud as he neared his truck. Breathing in the sweet, ripe smell of the peaches, he squatted down to pick one up. He dusted it off on his pants, and then examined it. The peach was perfect, unbruised and whole. Who was he to interfere with the timing of another person's life? He bit into the flesh, eating his way around the pit, taking one slow, deliberate bite after another.

THE SWEEPERS

CLARK PRACTICALLY lived in his father's recliner since Sylvie had left town. This was where he ate half-baked pepperoni pizzas, checked his email, and watched reruns of *Seinfeld* and *The Office* and *Law & Order* for hours at a time. This was where he came when the electric thrum of his pain kept him awake at night. It was here that he escaped the locker-room stench of his bedroom and the feeling of being watched. Here, he felt alone, not himself exactly, but unencumbered by the person he had once been. The warm leather held his body like a hand in a glove. When he shifted, which was often, the chair released a pleasant kissing sound. These days it was the only place he could get comfortable, even if the feeling was fleeting.

He'd been off the painkillers since he'd come home from the hospital in Santa Cruz. He was irritable. It was difficult to sleep. The encounter with Ned's parents haunted him and the thought of Joelle made him sick to his stomach. He continued to see people out his window—children asking for chocolate and men wearing dishdasha and white prayer caps. They gave him menacing looks and then disappeared as quickly as they appeared. Before she left town, he'd lost it with Sylvie.

He wore what had served for the last six years as his pajamas: a long-sleeved cross-country jersey and a pair of nylon running shorts. In high school, he'd found it easier to start each morning's six mile run if he woke already dressed. His legs were now thin and unused, ugly with scabs. His muscles ached from atrophy. He had no idea that it would hurt so much to shrink. His physical therapist insisted he was improving. Still, he ran out of breath walking to the mailbox and back or climbing into the truck cab. Although he hated his legs to be touched or looked at, he'd started wearing the shorts because everything else rubbed against the scabs. With Sylvie gone, there was no reason to care.

It was just after four in the morning. His father, disturbed by yesterday's train accident on one of his crossings, had slept as lightly as Clark. Clark could hear him shuffle to the upstairs bathroom, the toilet flush, and then his softened footsteps on the stairs. He waited for his father to step through the living room on his way to the kitchen where he'd heat up some milk in the microwave and then sit down to watch television with Clark, neither of them saying a word.

The Remington, pungent with solvents, leaned against the wall beside Clark's chair, glistening in the muted television's glow. Clark made no attempt to hide it. Earlier in the evening, watching the local news coverage of the train accident, Clark had braced the rifle between his scarred knees and put a patch over the hole, plunging the barrel with the rod. He wondered how many disturbed crossings he and Ned had helped to clear? How many decimated cars had they seen? How many torn-up bodies? In the background of the news coverage, the railroad company's spokesman calmly conferred with the county deputies. This was not how it was done in Iraq. There, the devastation started a chain reaction of wailing that could not be contained. This seemed to Clark much more honest. It was how he felt inside.

Clark's back was to the door, but he could see his father's reflection on the television screen as he stood in the entryway. Why didn't he walk in? Did he think Clark was asleep? To prove he wasn't, Clark flipped through the television stations. More crap: a sapphire ring rotated in its velvet box, a man in a white apron shoved tomatoes and carrots down the long throat of a juicer. Counting the crunches along with the guy using an ab reducer, Clark dared his father to step in and ask about the gun in plain sight. After returning from his mother's, he'd taken it from his father's truck. The quiet that he'd once taken for granted in the house had become a threatening void. When he couldn't sleep, he cleaned the gun. The methodical steps gave him purpose and the chemical smell made him feel safe.

Clark scratched at his legs, willing his father to speak. He lifted the lever beneath the armrest and shifted his weight so that the recliner tilted back another notch, lifting his legs and feet to eye level. He stared at the two meandering tracks of bruised scabs that started mid-shin and made their way up each of his legs to his shorts, forming a sort of farmer's tan of shrapnel wounds—boot top to hem— willing them to fade. These were what his mother yearned to see, what his father pretended not to see, all that Sylvie seemed to see.

"Worthless sacks of shit," he said out loud. "I wish I'd lost them." He kept going, waiting for his father to speak up and comfort him or tell him not to feel sorry for himself. Anything. "I wish I were dead," Clark said loudly.

When he looked up, his father's reflection was gone from the television screen. A few seconds later, the front door clicked open and then closed; a puff of cool air hit Clark's arm. Outside, his father revved the truck's engine a few times and drove off.

Alone again, Clark turned on the floor lamp and held up the worn envelope that had been sitting on the table beside him. Despite his promise those months ago, he still hadn't mailed it. Sometimes when he looked at the handwriting in a certain way, he could hear the dead woman's voice. It was almost a whisper. But the truth was she'd never spoken to him, never said a word. Clark had lied to Sylvie and his father. He had not found the letter in an old woman's apron, as he'd said, nor had the woman been dead, and, possibly the most egregious of the lies, he had never mailed the letter as he claimed he had. Her family must be searching for her, as all the while Clark held onto a clue that could have helped them know what had happened to her.

On the day Clark found the woman, nothing had been going right. Clark's squad had been sent to a neighborhood just beyond their usual jurisdiction—a market area known for its electronics that had been hit by a suicide bomb. They were called in as the second responders, the Sweepers, there to quantify the damage and organize cleanup efforts with the community. It was, in Army-speak, a reconnaissance and reconciliation mission, R & R. Using out-of-date maps, they'd gotten lost and were dependent on their translator, who they knew, but not well enough. Each street they turned down quickly became impassable. While backing out of a narrow passageway, they'd almost hit a Canadian tanker. Arriving late as strangers to the community, they would be starting off on the wrong foot.

Even the attack had been a screw up. The suicide bomber, losing his nerve, had unstrapped his backpack full of explosives at the corner of the market near a bus stop and music vendor and kept walking. Seven dead, twelve injured, one missing, not counting the bomber himself. Presumably he'd escaped. Presumably, he was a he.

Clark's company finally parked at the far edge of the market and radioed to the unit who was supposed to meet them for debriefing and a rundown on the neighborhood. Relieved to be on his own two feet, Clark strapped his rifle over his back and began to make his way with Tibbs and Lyons through the bustling market toward ground zero. Ned had been dead for a few weeks.

Clark had misplaced his sunglasses and the intense sunlight threatened a headache. They walked through the crowd cautiously, not speaking or stopping to touch the fabrics or sample the orange slices they were offered. Clark wondered what it meant for a young man hell-bent on paradise to lose his nerve like that. Where would he go? Had someone been watching him through a pair of binoculars? Would he have to disappear and pretend to be dead for the rest of his life? What had changed his mind—a book title on a bookseller's table, a pretty shop girl, a pastry on a cart?

A ways off, Clark could hear mourners. The three soldiers walked toward the wailing. Eventually the acrid smell of hot metal and melted plastic began to burn Clark's nostrils. They could see the damage: scattered brick, smoldering crates, collapsed tables, the burned-out shell of what looked to have been an electronics stall.

Because they were late, the hard work was already done. They stepped over the military's yellow caution tape toward a bent awning. Clark found the tape absurd. It should be wrapped around the whole country, the whole world, for that matter. The remaining tattered canopies shifted in a rare breeze. Finding so many goods destroyed—fruit and fabrics and books and the tiny boxes of travel alarm clocks and garish CDs—Clark was overcome with his own helplessness. In a place where people had lost so much, how could they do this to each other? Why not let Allah do the punishing?

A barefoot kid picked through the rubble, salvaging goods. The bus stop—what had been a cement shelter—was a mound. The pole that once listed bus schedules was twisted into a hangman's post. Next to a beat-up bus, two women embraced each other and sobbed. There was the expected shoe, a pair of headphones. In the dust, something shiny caught the sun and sparkled—sunglasses. Tibbs picked them up, looked into the mirror lenses, and then placed them on his head; Clark stepped away so he wouldn't have to acknowledge the theft.

He sat down on a pile of concrete blocks to wait for the first responders to give them the report. A call to prayer resounded from the speakers of a nearby mosque. He stacked up a few warped CD cases and then kicked them over, wondering, as he did more and more often since Ned's death, what difference it made that he was here. His mother had been right about this not being a place for him. If he were to admit it wholeheartedly, he would crumble. Behind him, something shifted beneath a tarp. A rat was Clark's first thought, except rats didn't cough. The second cough confirmed the first. Clark looked around to see if the others had heard. Except for the crying women and the boy, the area was deserted. Tibbs and Lyons were now out of sight. Was he imagining it? In all of his assignments, he'd never found anyone alive. He pulled at the rubble, pushing aside boards and burnt fabric, speaking calmly into the debris, "It's OK."

Tibbs appeared at a distance, walking in that awkward robotic way they all did when they had to pack so much gear. Lyons, sweat-drenched, was behind him, deep in conversation with two Marines. None of them noticed Clark at work. Through the wreckage, he recognized a man's bloodied back. The missing person, he assumed, finding no pulse on the neck. But there was the cough again. And then Clark saw a light-blue sleeve, coated in dust and blood, beneath the dead man's body. A woman's battered hand moved slightly. There was the cough again. Clark pulled off a large piece of plywood and threw it to the side. The man's crushed and bloody limbs were collapsed around hers as if he'd tried to protect her. Clark knew he should call out to the others for help. Instead, he whispered, "I'll save you," as he continued to pull away the debris, one small piece of cement at a time.

It took some maneuvering to reveal her face. Her eyes opened wide and then closed against the light. She blinked a few times, attempted to lift her head and then groaned. Clark shook his head, quieting her. She seemed to be near his age. Blood trickled from her nose. She coughed again and more blood surfaced at her lips and then fell back down into her mouth. Her breathing was a shallow, mucus-filled wheeze. The fact that she hadn't choked yet gave Clark hope. He reached through the tangle of debris to touch her cheek. Her left side was crushed; what he could see of her leg looked oddly bent above a pool of blood. Her lips were already tinted blue. Clark needed to clear her passageway, but mangled pipes pinned her in. It would take four men to lift the bricks to get her out. She would die watching them.

Although she must have been in excruciating pain, she grabbed his hand and tried to guide it between her body and the dead man's. Believing she was disturbed by the dead body on top of her, Clark attempted to lift the man off, but she grabbed Clark's hand again, shoving it further in, between the two bodies into what seemed to be a large pocket. Clark grasped at the pocket's contents. The first thing he touched was distinctly human, a child, he thought, as he jerked his hand out to find a tangle of gray and black hair. She shook her head, her eyes persistent. She wanted to give him something. He reached in again. It felt like touching a wild animal's nest. Something sharp jabbed his hand—a claw, a beak, scissors he realized—and then he felt it nestled in the hair—paper, an envelope. When he grabbed it, her lips pressed into a smile. He slid it out, tucked it into his vest, and then gently set his hand on hers. "I'll send it for you," he whispered before calling out to Tibbs and Lyons and the Marines. Her eyes looked into his. They were peaceful and sure, no longer showing any pain.

It was now seven in the morning, the sun out and songbirds chirping like mad. His father hadn't returned from wherever he'd gone. For a long time, Clark had been admiring the feminine script on the envelope. He believed he could tell a lot about people from their handwriting. For instance, his father's was jagged and small, like bird prints in dirt, skittery in the way his father could be. Sylvie's letters were full and round, hopeful and ripe. Even the letter he'd received from her yesterday, telling him that she didn't want him anymore, used those happy letters. Clark thought he could recognize her relief in the way she'd signed her name with the tail of the *e* at the end wagging itself off the page. It looked like a Frisbee in midair, and the letter made the same gesture as he tossed it into the kitchen garbage can. His own handwriting was neat, with a deliberate tilt to the left even though he was right-handed. Once he'd thought it demonstrated his lack of conformity. Now, he was pretty sure he was like everyone else—everyone else, that is, who'd gone to war and come back. On the other hand, this woman's handwriting was light and careful, like her touch. It reminded him of her thin, cold fingers, bruised and bloodied, the perfect ovals of her nails.

Clark turned off *The Morning Show* and levered himself to a seated position so that his feet could touch the floor. His legs had gone numb again. Pulling himself up to standing, he knocked down his father's rifle in the process. It embarrassed him to remember how he'd hurt and frightened Sylvie with the gun.

The argument started with a seduction gone wrong. "You need to get help," Sylvie said gently when he'd gotten defensive.

"Just let it go," Clark answered, pulling the sheets up and picking up the freshly cleaned gun so he could aim it out the window. He wasn't sure what was more pathetic: the skinny dot-to-dot of his legs or his shriveled dick. He turned to Sylvie. "Besides, the doctors say I'm getting better."

"I'm not talking about your knee—or your rib. You've gotten even more internal lately. What just happened is a sign of depression." Sylvie dressed as she spoke, hooking her bra in the back, with her elbows out at the side and her breasts pushed forward like a proud bird. "You need to talk to someone, a professional."

With these words, Clark ordered her to shut up, thrusting the rifle barrel into her stomach like a pointed finger. A reflex. She fell back. When Clark saw the fear in her eyes, so much like the look in Joelle's the night Ned woke her in the women's quarters, he rushed to the kitchen and grabbed ice.

Reading Sylvie's letter yesterday, he'd felt respect for her as well as relief. She'd been able to do what he, for months now, could not. He was proud of her for boldly stating the truth: she didn't love him anymore. Strangely, the words made him feel less alone, as if he'd been lost for a long time and had finally seen smoke in the distance, friend or foe, he didn't know, but another living soul for sure. There was one less lie to tell, one less person to let down.

In the kitchen, he took a stamp from his father's bill-paying stash and four Ibuprofens. He placed the stamp on the corner of the woman's envelope and then licked the tissue-thin flap to seal it. It tasted of glue, dust, and sweat: Iraq. He went upstairs and found a pair of socks and old running shoes. They were surprisingly lightweight but ill-fitting, as if they'd been formed to someone else's feet. Bending to tie the laces was hell, but he got through it. He found an old fanny pack in his closet and strapped it to his waist, zipping the letter in with a shaky hand.

It had been a long time since he'd stepped outside for longer than a few minutes. It was still early. The air was cool, but it was going to be a hot day. Since Sylvie had been gone, he'd kept his curtains drawn. He searched the sides of the house for Iraqis, telling himself not to look afraid. At the edge of the driveway, Clark swung his arms around to loosen up. His shoulder joints popped. He turned his head from one side to the other, jogging in place for a few seconds, getting used to the impact. His legs were weak, wobbly even, but it felt good to use them in the old way, even as a series of sharp pains—first from the meniscus and then from the newest of the shrapnel zits—shot through them. He felt more clear-headed than he had in a long time.

He saluted the faded plastic owl perched over the empty garage, which he noticed needed a paint job. When had the place started to fall into such disrepair? He told himself that today when he got home from the post office he would strip the garage while listening to one of those radio stations that plays Top 40 from a decade ago. He would water the lawn. He would clean out his room. Do a load of laundry. The list continued as he stepped slowly out on the road.

After a few yards, he started focusing ahead, letting his legs paddle the asphalt, doing his best to ignore the pain each step hammered in. He remembered his former self, running through exhaustion to cross the finish line. The fanny pack bounced lightly on his hips. He stuck to the gravel shoulder, running toward traffic as he'd done so many mornings in the past. It was strange to be out. Strange to be alone and out. Strange to be back in a world that was at once familiar and foreign. How far from the road these houses were. How tall the pines. How bright and insistent every color seemed to be—the painted houses, the pine needles, the morning sun.

Bees already buzzed around in the high grass skirting the shoulder. His uncle had died in a spot like this just a month before Clark's return. While away, it had felt as if the death was yet another casualty of war, a part of his deployment. Now, running along the ditch with its yellowing grasses and cattails and the occasional discarded coffee cup, the permanence of his uncle's absence hit him. Clark tried to regulate his breath. It was important that he keep going. If he were to stop, he would never get there. Up the road, a tan SUV drove toward him. Clark's heart and legs sped up, a built-in response to get away. Passing by, the driver waved as if it were all a joke.

Clark knew each mile marker from their house into the small town and beyond. The train tracks were about a half mile from home —time to kick it in on the return as he remembered his junior high coach yelling near the finish line at cross-country meets. At the first railroad crossing, Clark was relieved to find no cars, no flashing lights. He held his breath and sped across. His father must be blaming himself for yesterday's accident. He was a man encased in guilt. For years, Clark had been trying to let his father know that he—they— were OK.

The O'Farrells' gray barn marked the mile. Crossing their driveway, Clark realized he hadn't paced himself. Stomach cramps and the residual tenderness of his healed rib were making it difficult to breathe. He slowed to a shuffle, turning down a side road where the field had been recently sliced into subdivisions. The high school was up the road a ways, but the post office was still a good mile from here. A protective starling dive-bombed him from an old apple tree. Clark tripped. His legs throbbed as if all of his blood had rushed down to them and couldn't find its way back.

He felt light-headed and his throat was dry. The shifting brush on the side of the road seemed to be chastising him. He tried to quiet his footsteps, but his limp had returned with its one-two thud. In the distant field, a figure emerged, actually two: an old woman in a abaya carrying a child on her back. The child was too large to be carried and his legs almost touched the ground. When Clark stopped to get a better look, they hid in the shadows of an outbuilding. His heart raced, high up near his throat and ears, making it difficult to swallow the thick phlegm that had accumulated in his mouth. He hacked up a loogie and spat, steadying himself. He unbelted the fanny pack and slung it over his shoulder as if it were a rifle so he could keep himself on track. "Post office," he repeated to himself under his breath.

A few minutes later, a pickup truck heading toward him slowed. Clark slipped down the shoulder and took cover, steadying himself against a mailbox post to watch as the truck turned into the large parking lot of Saint Maria's Church across the street. A man climbed out of the cab, pulled a bucket and broom out of the truck bed, and then unlocked one of the church's double-doors with a key from a large ring. Clark couldn't see his face, but his hair was nearly black, his skin tan.

Clark felt trapped. This stranger seemed more real than the others. He looked down the long gravel driveway that started at the mailbox where he was crouched and ended a distance up at a one-story ranch house. It was white with a wrought-iron rail leading toward the door. No one appeared to be home. Clark considered and then rejected the impulse to fish the letter out of his fanny pack and stick it into the mailbox and call it a day, mission accomplished. The plan didn't feel sure enough: Clark needed to know that the letter would get into the mail. Out of city limits, people could be sticklers about their private property. Seeing the letter in his mailbox, especially with the Arabic lettering, the guy who lived here—Cameron, the box said—might burn it or turn it in to the post office and have an official open it. Clark couldn't stand to think of the violation. Even after months carrying it around, he'd never pulled the letter from the envelope.

"You, there," came a voice from across the street. Clark froze, grabbed the narrow pack hanging from his shoulder. None of the figures he'd seen in the past had ever spoken to him. "You OK?" this one asked without an accent.

Clark stood and climbed the ditch toward the road. "Just taking a leak," Clark lied. "I was on my way into town."

"I could drive you," the man offered.

"That's OK," Clark said, feeling exhausted. The pain in his legs was now compounded with the sting of the shallow scratches from the dry grass.

"It's no problem."

Clark resisted, but the man wouldn't give in. "It's always further than it seems it should be. It's no trouble."

In the woods behind the man, a shadow shifted.

"You sure?" Clark asked.

"Let's go," the guy said in answer.

Clark crossed the street and met him at his truck. He climbed in. A bucket of cleaners and wet rags sat at his feet. He finally fully comprehended that the man was from here, not there.

"That your church?" Clark asked as they pulled out of the lot.

"Since I was a kid. But my favorite time to be inside is when it's empty. Like today. Just me and God. What about you? What are you doing out so early?" The guy smiled so that his dark moustache tilted like a soaring bird. He was in his forties and lean with a long, angular face.

"Thought I'd take a jog."

"I always hated running."

"I used to be a lot better, that's for sure."

"What happened there?" He gestured toward Clark's legs.

They were a mess—scratched and scarred. One of his shrapnel scabs had opened up, the blood trailing down his shin. Here was one of those moments when he could lie, be vague, or just tell it. Clark wiped his sweaty forehead on his arm. He didn't know this guy. It didn't matter.

"IED," Clark finally said.

"Shit, you're a vet?"

"I guess so."

"You're so young." The man kept his eyes on the road, thrusting his chin into the air above the steering wheel as he talked. "Afghanistan?" he asked.

"Iraq."

"Grant," the guy said, holding out his hand. "Where are we headed exactly?"

"The post office."

The two talked for a while and then Grant, who had two daughters at the same junior high that Clark had attended, asked how old he was.

"Nineteen," Clark answered.

"Old enough to die for the country, but not have a drink."

"Heard that one before."

"What's next for you?"

Clark shrugged.

"Have a job?"

"My family wants me to go to school," Clark answered, watching the houses go by outside the window. Clark thought he saw someone or something, or maybe even a dog, step behind an empty boat trailer.

"And you?" Grant asked.

"It's something I've always assumed I'd do, but now I doubt I'd fit in."

They turned onto the short commercial drag. At the Mennonite bakery, Grant stopped as a group of bonneted women crossed the street. He rolled down the window and took a deep breath.

Grant's chin gestured toward the women. "What about you—are you a believer?" he asked Clark.

"No," Clark answered without hesitation, thinking of the soldiers who wore saints around their necks, the ones who carried good luck tokens, the ones who studied Tae Kwon Do or refused to change their socks. They had rituals and a logic they could apply to loss, someone larger than themselves they could turn to, even blame. They had ways to refocus the pain. He imagined himself inside the sanctuary of the big Catholic church, dust motes drifting through the sunrays that funneled through the golden skylight, his feet sinking into the plush red carpet as he approached the sinewy, bloody body of a plaster Christ. What was there to say?

As the truck bounced over a silent crossroad, the broom in the bed rolled from one side to the other, and the red cinderblock post office came into view. Grant switched on his blinker and the cab filled with the quick tick-tock that reminded Clark of a faucet drip. He'd always loved the sound of the blinker, the clearly stated intention to turn or switch lanes, and then the final click as the wheel fulfilled its assignment. Grant pulled up next to a postbox and Clark climbed out of the truck.

"I can make it home," Clark told him through the window.

"You sure about that?"

"I needed the rest, but I'm good now."

Grant reached his hand out again, and with a deep sincerity in his voice, shook Clark's hand. "Thank you for what you did over there. You'll be in my prayers."

"Thanks," Clark replied, embarrassed. He watched Grant drive away. It seemed too easy to create a myth, a hero, something to believe in. He'd done that once himself with Ned, but he'd never be that gullible again.

Clark unzipped the fanny pack and pulled out the letter. Everyone had taken mementos from Iraq: rings and watches, teeth and gory photographs. For a long time, the letter had been it for him, proof. Once he let go of the letter, the only memento he would have from his tour in Iraq would be his legs. A knot tightened in his throat. If he'd called out immediately after discovering the trapped woman, could they have released her from the rubble in time? He would never know.

Clark opened the postbox door and dropped the letter into the darkness, remembering the way the woman's eyes held his as she died. In the back of his mind, something went off—a scream, an explosion.

It hadn't taken as long as Clark imagined to clear the area around the woman where the bomb had gone off. They laid both of the corpses out on the ground on cloth and then covered them, searching the area for other remains. Among the smashed CDs and sheets of music, they found a backpack with spray-paint cans and the remnants of an anatomy book in English. The young man, apparently a vendor in the market, had his ID card dutifully tucked into his pocket. The young woman had little to identify her except the scissors, an apron pocket full of hair, and a university identification card they'd found near the anatomy book. The two mourners claimed the young man as their nephew and cousin, but when asked about the young woman, their eyes fell and they shook their heads in adamant denial. They didn't know her.

"Maybe she's who we're looking for," Lyons said, thrusting his gun toward the unidentified corpse. Sweat dripped down his forehead and onto the ground.

"What do you mean?" Tibbs asked.

"We're near the epicenter. Maybe she's a lady suicide."

"Lost her huevos," a Marine quipped.

"More than that," said the other.

Everyone except Clark laughed. He knelt down and uncovered her face, studying it in the sunlight, crusted with blood and dust, trying to imagine her alive. She wore tiny gold hoops in her ears and leather shoes. Her university was far from here and she looked too well-off to live in this district. Did she know the man who had been buried with her? Clark and Tibbs lifted her body onto a handheld stretcher along with the possible identification and then pushed it through the double doors of the military ambulance. For the first time, Clark slipped her letter out of his pocket. There was an Arabic name, but an American address. Lyons's words—lady suicide— went through his mind. He wondered if he should turn the letter over to his superiors, but thought better of it. If she was the suicide bomber, he didn't want anyone to know.

By the time Clark reached the train tracks, day had begun. Police tape stretched across both sides of the gate. His father's truck was pulled up next to the crossing, but Clark didn't see him. Drawing closer, the buzz of flies became audible. He stepped on something soft and breathed in a familiar, fragrant smell—peaches. The ground was thick with them. They must have been on the truck that had been hit by the train.

Clark spotted a man on his hands and knees beyond the yellow barrier, dragging a broken crate beside him and filling it with the fruit. Clark watched, almost distrustful. He wondered if this was yet another disappearing figure. The man dusted off a peach on his shoulder and set it carefully into the crate. Clark cautiously stepped closer. "Dad?" he whispered, setting his hand on the man's shoulder.

His father looked up, startled, his face dust-covered and wet around his nose and mouth. "Son?" he said, his breath sweet with peaches. "Is that you?" He stood, squinting at Clark in disbelief, and then touched Clark's arm as if to make sure he was real. He looked down at his son's legs and frowned.

"It's OK," Clark said, stepping backward and nodding to the crate. "What are you doing out here?"

"Cleaning," his father answered, kneeling back down. "I hate to see all of these wasted."

Clark attempted to squat. Halfway down he lost his footing and fell onto the ground. He could already feel the lactic acid from his earlier run tightening up his muscles, accelerating the ache. He reached out for a peach and then another, setting them carefully into the box.

"Did you follow me here?" his father asked.

"I had to mail something."

"Ah, a reply to Sylvie?"

Ignoring the optimism in his father's voice, Clark replied, "We're over."

His father cleared his throat. "I'm sorry to hear that."

Clark tossed a damaged peach toward the tracks. "She's better off without me."

"No, she isn't," his father said quietly. "None of us would be."

They filled the crate with more peaches than the two of them could ever eat. Clark selected one from the top, dusted it off on his jersey, and took a bite. The first bite was gritty, but the second was possibly the best he'd ever had. The sweetness reminded him of a moment from childhood. Snow out the window. A spoonful of pudding. It was a moment from before, as his mother once put it, before the memory was inexplicably stripped of its innocence.

Each carrying a side of the crate, father and son climbed over the police tape and headed to the truck. As they drove home, country music playing on the radio, Clark considered the letter in the mail, finally traveling to its intended. He watched out the side window as the lots grew larger and the houses further from the road. First one and then another Arab figure emerged in the fields and then slipped out of view. He wondered who they were—snipers seeking cover, kids kicking around a soccer ball, a nursing mother. He wondered if they were people he'd seen before, strangers his mind had taken in and stored for dreams, people he'd helped or hurt. Whoever they were, Clark suspected they would always be there, like the shrapnel in his legs and the shame. Resting his arm out the truck window, he peered into the rearview mirror to see what the figures turned into once he'd passed by them—mailboxes, scarecrows, horses maybe, or deer—and was surprised to recognize the reflection of his own face staring back at him.

III

ALIVE

WHEN THE letter arrived Jamal was slogging through the final pages of an article on the intermingling of European languages in North Africa as he downed cheese puffs from a bag. To do this while reading was an art, and he was careful not to let his lips touch his fingertips. He sighed out loud and turned the page. Jamal despised post-colonial theory just as much as Professor Vann seemed to despise him. The study of colonialism, no matter how critical, never failed to make the people in question appear weak and unaccountable. Seated in a sunny rental on West Huron Street, two miles from the state university where Jamal studied and taught Arabic poetry thousands of miles from its source, he felt all too familiar with the way one language or culture could overcome another. Working through his advisor's reading list, Jamal felt accused—not of domination, but of submission.

He pulled at the couch's batik slipcover and wiped his orange fingertips on the backside, wondering if Vann recognized in him something of his own German soul that he had been taught to hate. Jamal knew his own family hadn't suffered under President Hussein. In fact, his father, a poet and calligrapher, once worked at the palace, inscribing invitations to events for Arab dignitaries and providing superficial quotations for banners. Only once did Jamal's father compose something original for the president: a minor poem about spring that he gave as a gift to his first wife. Jamal knew that from the start, the job had disheartened his father, who eventually found work at a private high school in a middle-class Baghdad neighborhood. That was years ago, even before the first American attacks, when Jamal and Leila were children.

Although Jamal knew his father had succeeded in distancing himself from the president while providing a sheltered life for his family, he'd been unable to protect them from the current war. Professor Vann had no idea about the suffering of Jamal's family—how one morning four months earlier, just days before his sister Leila was to leave for Cairo, she left home for work and never returned. Every day, Jamal's father searched for her in hospitals, prisons, graveyards, and morgues, rushing to suicide bomb sites, every week revising and sending in a new description of her to the Bureau of Missing Persons. Only Jamal's mother, whispering tearfully into the phone, acknowledged what Jamal also now believed. His sister was dead. Jamal had told no one, not his roommates, the anthropologists Dave and Pete; not Marli, the undergrad architect who snuck into his bedroom several nights a week; and certainly not Professor Vann. Leila's disappearance felt abstract, too difficult to explain, and so Jamal remained silent. There was no way for him to say her name in the past tense.

Reading Arabic poetry was his only true comfort. In Leila's absence, Arabic had become more than a language for him; it was the place where his sister still existed. He enjoyed its form, the way in which the alphabet was more than a representation of sound, but also a suggestion of feeling. When inscribed by hand as their father had taught them, it was psychological, the act of writing as essential and alive as speaking, each letter shaped by what had come before. On the page, the white areas weren't simply empty spaces to be ignored, but intricate rooms shaped by the walls of script, an invitation to be near Leila.

Realizing that his mind had wandered once again to Leila, Jamal focused his eyes back onto the page and tried to concentrate on the English. He was finally making progress when Pete rushed through the front door and dropped an envelope facedown onto Jamal's lap.

He could tell instantly by its weight and shape that it was a letter from home. His father, no doubt, writing something important: do not be tempted by riches, do not be seduced by drugs, do not succumb to violence, there is no reason to return home, son. These carefully worded letters, arriving increasingly often, saddened Jamal. He imagined his grieving father up late worried by some bit of gruesome news of America presented by one of the beautiful newscasters on Al Jazeera. Not looking forward to reading it, Jamal took the time to suck the cheddar dust from his fingertips before slowly folding over the bag of cheese puffs and gathering his reading into a stack. Debating with himself whether it would be wrong to put off his father's letter for a few hours, he turned over the envelope.

Recognizing Leila's handwriting, his heart skipped a beat and then sped up. His tongue caught along the sides of his mouth, which were unbearably dry. Although he felt as if he'd been stabbed in the chest, he managed to yell casually down the hall, "Thanks, Pete," before stumbling into his room and pushing the door shut with his shoulder. He slipped his trembling fingers under the envelope's seal, leaving orange smudges along the margins, as he unfolded her letter.

What came next was a jumble for Jamal. He rebuked himself for having ever believed that his sister was dead, yet felt reluctant to read the words on the page, as if the letter itself were his sister and to read it would be to erase her. For a short while, it was enough to hold the letter as if it were her hand. Relishing the thought, tears filled his eyes. It had happened before—a yearning so deep for his twin that he could feel her close, searching for him in the vast Midwestern night or just on the other side of his bedroom wall. He should never have listened to his father who worried too much about his son's studies and safety. He should have returned to Baghdad, to her. He wondered, then, why his parents hadn't called him yet with the extraordinary news of her return. There was no logic to it. Still standing at his door, he read the letter. Too quickly, it ended.

He turned the envelope over in his hands. There was no actual return address, only an American stamp and a postmark from Deer Park, Washington. He paused, taking it in. Was it possible that she was not home, but here, on the same continent as he was, in the same country, and that his parents did not know? The postal date was two days before. Her proximity took his breath away. He held the proof in his hands, yet could not believe it.

He sat down on his bed. Smoothing the letter open in his lap, he read it again slowly, savoring his sister's every word, listening to what she was trying to tell him. Leila's beautiful script conveyed the scent of rose water and the lilt of her voice as she gave news from home, much of which he already knew. Then she started to whisper, confiding in him, revealing a weighty secret that at once explained her disappearance and created a new void. She'd lied to their parents and acted without discretion, putting herself in harm's way. This was not the Leila that Jamal knew, yet there was no hint at apology, only excessive happiness. Joy.

A twinge of their old rivalry jabbed at Jamal along with the urge to protect someone's honor, although he wasn't sure if it was his family's, his sister's, or his own. Tucked into the envelope was a lock of black hair, the same color and texture as hers—and his. Finally, she had found him. He needed to get to her before it was too late.

At the graduate library, Jamal researched Deer Park, a small town on the eastern edge of Washington state. It had two high schools and a golf course, a number of grocery stores and churches and bars, a florist, and a small private airport. Commercial planes flew into Spokane, a city named for a Native American tribe. Deer Park was 2,000 miles away from Ann Arbor, 33 hours by car, 6 by plane. Jamal tried not to dwell on the fact that the letter never mentioned any of this, that Leila had stated specifically that she'd spent the week in Baghdad, that Leila wanted to study medicine and this place, Deer Park, had no university. If he were to go to Deer Park, how would he find her? How would he start? He imagined himself waking in a motel, mapping out imaginary days searching for her, and then their reunion. But, when someone was searching for you, wasn't the rule to simply stay put?

From the stacks, Jamal watched Marli scan returns for an emeritus. She often complained about the "geezers" who had a tendency to condescend whenever she explained that the outdated books they couldn't find in the stacks had been relocated to the silverfish-infested bowels of the library where couriers were sent to retrieve them. With fearful admiration, Jamal watched the no-nonsense, brutish way Marli handled the stack of musty books, pressing them wide open like a butcher halving a bird carcass, before she rushed them across the sensors and tossed them into the bin. She seemed to take an interest in one and set it aside. When she concentrated, her tongue rested on her upper lip. Between stacks, she took a swig from a take-out coffee cup. Wondering if she ever thought of him when he was not around, he grabbed a book from the shelf and approached.

"Hey," she said, apparently pleased to see him. When he reached the circulation desk, she took the book from his hand and read the spine: *Popular Mechanics*, 1982. "Are you stalking me?" she asked, her lips turned up mockingly.

She stepped out from behind the counter, rescued an abandoned book cart, and started rolling it down the aisle toward the far windows, scooping up the bound periodicals that had been abandoned on the long metal shelves. Jamal followed, setting the book on top. If anyone could help him find his sister in this huge country, it would be Marli.

"What are you doing tonight?" he asked.

She blew air through her lips so they vibrated. "A final project due Tuesday. I might get it done if I work straight through. So much for an easy summer class. What about you?"

Alive / 169

On a shelf above her head, a bright-blue wad of gum hovered. Standing there in the narrow aisle, Jamal almost had to look up at her. She was tall for a girl, graceful with her long neck. It didn't make sense that after all this time he would finally open up to her or ask her for help, but nothing about his relationship with her made sense. "Why me?" he'd once asked her, but now he couldn't remember her response.

"Pete and Dave are having a party," he said.

"Sounds fun," she said sarcastically. "Are you here to invite me?"

"Would you come?" he asked, hopefully.

Marli answered with an American, noncommittal shrug.

With her, he had always been passive, following her lead so as not to have to claim responsibility for his actions. What they had was physical—from the fingernails-on-chalkboard cringe he felt when she touched the lines of poetry he'd written in his notebook to the way their bodies tangled and bumped into each other on the nights she tapped at his window. In the morning, she slipped out of his room like a thief, disappearing just as suddenly as she had appeared to him late one night when he was walking home from studying in Rackham. When he'd explained that he was a graduate student in Near Eastern Studies, she said, "Good, you'll never be my TA," giving him a firm handshake as if they'd just signed a contract. In the weeks they'd been together, he had never been to her house or taken her to a restaurant, never called her on her cell phone. His sister's letter made him wonder if things could be different. Could Marli make him complete?

"You could meet my roommates," he offered.

"You've told me enough about them. Besides, I don't like the way graduate students act around undergrads. They're either lecherous or extremely patronizing."

"I'll protect you."

"See what I mean?" She leaned in and planted a kiss on his lips in front of everyone: two students hunched over a laptop in a nearby carrel and an elderly patron carrying a leather valise toward the counter. Her carelessness frightened him. The smell of musty books and the taste of coffee on her breath reminded him of home and the tea houses on Mutanabbi Street. In March, it had been blown to smithereens.

"My sister wrote me," he blurted out.

Marli stepped back, smiling and shaking her head. She pressed her finger into his chest. "I knew you had a sister, I could tell. You're so tender." She put her hands on the sides of his cheeks and looked into his eyes as if she were older and wiser than he would ever be. "Why haven't you said anything about her?"

"She lives in Washington," he said, trying on the idea.

"That explains it. Everyone in DC works for the CIA. Is she another Valerie Plame? Is it against the law to talk about her?" Marli teased, offering up yet another series of cultural references that he could not decode quickly enough.

"I could tell you about her tonight," he said, unhappy to hear the pleading tone in his voice.

"Maybe," she answered. "A bunch of us from class were think-ing of getting together if we finished our models—an incentive plan."

Marli often talked about her architectural models—the use of positive and negative space, the balance of function and fit, move-ment and stasis, the marriage of form and materials—but he'd never seen them. She was confident, but what if she was wrong about herself? He imagined describing her to his sister. Marli, with her headbands and perfect white teeth. Marli, whose fingers sometimes peeled with rubber cement and whose light-green thong once emerged from her backpack tangled in a geometry triangle. Marli, with her boyish breasts that flattened when she lay on her back and her entic-ing little belly button that pinched in like a keyhole. Marli, who traced Arabic letters backwards no matter how many times he told her his language read from right to left. Her response always the same: like Hebrew and driving in England. Marli was like America: unapologetic, addictive as cheese puffs. Jamal simultaneously felt drawn to and repelled by her, and while thinking about her during the day, a shameful amount of lust.

That night as he waited for Marli, Jamal read his sister's letter countless times, dissecting it as if it were a Lacanian text. Try as he might, he couldn't make sense of it. There was a vague mention of leaving Baghdad, but no explicit destination. Was she referring to Cairo or Deer Park? He tried to imagine Leila drinking mint tea at a wood-paneled café, surrounded by new friends—laughing American girls like Marli—who lifted her heavy dark hair and told her she was beautiful, surprised that she did not wear a hijab. She would touch another girl's hair, a blonde or a redhead, and explain that she could cut it as well as any of the expensive places. He could hear Leila laugh, not at the girls, but at him, bemused at his inability to understand. He stared at the pages in his hand, sure there was a simple explanation that he was overlooking. Once he understood better, he could call his parents.

The evening progressed and the party outside his door gradually grew louder as feet stomped up the wood porch and the doorbell rang. Every once in a while, a stranger peeked into Jamal's room to ask where the bathroom was located or where to put a backpack. With each interruption, Jamal looked up from his sister's letter, pointed toward Dave's room, and then started at the beginning again. Something about it was not right.

Dear Brother,

I'm sorry for the lapse. There is so little to say that I have not already said. In only a few days, I will be writing from a new place so I'm trying to take it all in. The sun is low and clear, with little smoke in the air, a relief. It has been a relatively peaceful week: chemistry in the mornings with Dr. Alousi who makes even brain waves dull. After that, I walk to the salon. Old lady Hadal came in again today to say her goodbyes. She comes so often, she will soon have no hair to cut. Sometimes I simply trim the air beneath her ends. I noticed another frightening bruise, this one above her eye. Although I know it is unkind, I wish her husband would hurry up to the grave. It is unfair to ask a woman to live so long with the shame of a public secret. Nothing I say can dissuade her from paying full price, and I must always stop short of insisting so as not to offend. Like so many in her generation (Papa among them), she sees generosity as pity. Sometimes, I admit, as I pull the comb through her thin hair as gently as I can, it is difficult to separate the two.

Sadly, I have heard that Hakim from your soccer days was killed at a checkpoint. His mother told me. I did not ask the circumstances, but there was something in the way she held her eyes that suggested shame as well as sorrow. I know you will deny caring, but I should also let you know that Aisha is engaged! Her husband-to-be is that distant cousin who lived in Australia for several years before returning to help his parents emigrate. Some would call this fate.

These repeated accounts from home must seem dull, but this has been my life without you—admittedly not so different from when you were here, except now there is no one to complain to, no one with the same references. Yet writing you in Michigan, imagining the vastness of the big lake you once described, I feel the desire to tell you everything—small and large.

In fact, I can put it off no longer: I am in love, Jamal! So strange to write. So strange to believe. Papa and Mum do not, must not, know. Not yet. Let me emphasize this. I can't tell you how many times I have begun this letter to you, but today is different. Today I will mail this off!

Maybe you have already guessed. He is not Ba'ath, or educated. He is not suitable for me in any of the acceptable ways, but there is a trust and a completeness I feel only in his presence. With him, even my boring life—my studies, my hours cutting hair, the days I am stuck inside—have meaning. We meet in the crowds of Shorjah where he sells CDs. When there are no customers, he sketches and paints, and I study. I take taxis to be with him whenever I can. In fact, I am with him now, seated on a fruit crate as he paints my portrait on a tucked away wall! He says it is his way of keeping me near when I am gone.

What can I tell you about him to make you understand—because, Jamal, I can already feel your disapproval. Know this, we have done nothing wrong. If you write to say you are happy for me, I will tell you his name. For now, let this be an introduction.

Although he has never studied formerly, he knows painting the way you and Father know poetry. I was with him when he sold his first small piece. This is connected to how we met, but I will save that for another letter. He is always sketching, his paint-splattered hands moving swiftly in his journal as he stares contentedly at teapots, rooflines, me. He works in his aunt's music stall in Shorjah market. His parents and siblings were killed by the Americans in '91, but my gentle painter does not seek revenge. He paints his anger and wants only to be left alone. No one has ever admitted it, but our family is like that—always changing the subject—don't you agree? His cousin and aunt—who have taken to calling me "kitten"—have embraced me as one of their own. I wish you could meet them. Maybe you would be able to convince Papa that I am a good judge of character. For now, I "study" late, racing curfew home, bouncing over the pitted streets in taxis. I know my tardiness makes Papa terribly anxious, but I'm tired of waiting for my life to begin. Don't worry about my grades; I have kept them up for no other reason than to maintain my cover. Only my letter writing has suffered.

Now that I have tasted the sweetness of love, I want it for everyone: Mum and Papa, poor Mrs. Hadal, dull Dr. Alousi, and most of all, you. Do you lift your eyes from your books long enough to notice any interesting girls? I believe Papa, while strict with me, would be much more supportive of your decision if you were to meet someone in Michigan. Mum and I worry that you are lonely. Tell me about your comings and goings. What do you eat? Do you still run the loop toward the dam and back? I imagine still water, carp swimming close to the surface, something like the marble fountain where we once played in the palace park. Have you convinced your cranky professor to leave you be?

Oh, how we miss you, Jamal, especially Papa who will not admit it, but has started to read Fawzi Karim. Maybe he is changing; maybe soon we will be able to speak about what we have lived through. Papa and I were talking the other day and we wanted to hear your opinion: is it possible to translate poetry from Arabic to English while keeping its deepest meaning? He is extremely proud of you. As for me, although I'm glad you are away from danger, I selfishly wish you were here. I need you now, older brother by four minutes, more than ever.

Please, please, twin, tell me you support me in this new, strange matter of love, the way I know I would support you.

In peace & with much love,

L

Growing up, they had been inseparable, always whispering and taunting, vying for their parents' love. Back then, they could guess what the other was thinking. When separated, they sought out each other. When together, they pushed the other away. With this letter, his sister was once again eluding him, reappearing to Jamal as mysteriously as she had disappeared. Even after reading and rereading the letter, Jamal felt no surer of anything. Had she eloped? Why was Leila here if her lover, if he could call him that, was in Iraq? Why would she come here rather than Cairo? Why had she gone to a state hovering on the furthest edge of the U.S. instead of directly to him? Why did the letter mention nothing of this new place? And then there was the secret she'd shared. If she were trying to tell him that she had eloped, then why would she bother to seek his approval? Searching the letter for answers, he found only questions that undermined the brief joy and relief that the letter had initially offered.

How could she make their parents suffer so long? Leila was asking too much of him. They deserved to know. Jamal tried to imagine a way to inform them without betraying Leila's confidence. Their mother, always the more understanding one, surely wouldn't be able to keep such a secret from their father. Before Jamal said anything to either of them, he needed to be sure. He returned the letter to his backpack and walked to the front of the house, scanning the rooms for Marli. The kitchen and back deck were packed with shaggy young men and clusters of women in flowing tops. The more they drank, the more they hugged. Jamal was still uncomfortable with such public intimacy, although everyone told him it meant nothing. The parties that he used to attend in Baghdad were never such casual events. There the women dressed up and the men wore shirts their mothers had ironed for them. Nights were filled with dancing and laughing and arguing about politics. Here the same thing happened, but it seemed that it was all a prelude for sex.

Jamal settled on the couch in the dim, deserted living room, studying the walls and shelves around him. A Bengali puppet—a horse with hooves made of bells—dangled from a sconce. On the mantel, a Japanese lacquer box held their fireplace matches and a baggie of pot that Jamal was not supposed to know about. A Turkish rug hung behind his head. The two anthropologists used their travel mementos to impress certain kinds of female graduate students who were mysteriously drawn to beards and hand-painted masks and loose-leaf teas. Already their plan was working. A petite woman with pink-tipped hair—like a paintbrush dipped in paint—moseyed in and lifted the blue cloth off the arm of the couch and asked, "Where do you think this beauty is from?"

Jamal shrugged. The fabric, while attractive, was always in need of rearranging, which served too much as a reminder of tousled linens and unmade beds and the messed-up, makeshift life Jamal had started in the U.S. along with his own cultural slippage. When Dave butted in to introduce the young woman, he said, "And this is Jamal," patting him on the shoulder as if he were yet another piece of exotica. "You'll never guess where he's from."

"Guantanamo," Jamal said, getting up. He downed another beer and then skirted the various party conversations: the complaints about funding and the job market, Obama versus Hillary, last-minute summer plans, the war and global warming. When he mentioned his studies, a few said "cool," but nothing more. Jamal wasn't sure if their responses were sparked by ignorance or embarrassment—by what they knew about his culture or what they did not know. In the past few months, things had been going poorly again in Baghdad. A minibus explosion, the murder of a state official, and now an increase in female suicide bombers. With this thought, Jamal, already three beers in, grabbed his jacket and was out the door before he knew where he was going.

He took West Washington toward downtown, past the Eight Ball and the Fleetwood and the Michigan Theater, ending up on South State Street, where, if he looked far enough into campus, he could make out the lit-up windows of the library where Marli worked. He wondered if she was there, but then remembered she'd mentioned getting together with the other architects. He headed down State and then onto South University, the undergraduate section of town. He immediately recognized Marli's bicycle with its fruit crate bungee-corded to the back parked next to a stack of shiny kegs at the side door of an undergraduate bar called The Brown Jug.

The ivy-covered patio was crowded, the indoor bar filled with guys younger than Jamal, their faces hidden below baseball caps, watching the Lions play the Yankees on the large-screen televisions that hung over the bar. A batter tapped the ground in front of home plate. The white bases made Jamal think of American tombstones. He made his way toward the counter and ordered a stout, squeezing in beside a couple thumb wrestling, their foreheads touching. As the foam settled, he looked around for Marli, unsure of what he would say if she asked him again if he was stalking her.

He spotted her at the side of the bar playing darts with a guy with the same dairy-induced, presidential good looks of so many of the university's undergrads. Marli was dressed up—as if she were on a date—in a tank top and a narrow flowered skirt. The round table behind them was loaded with stacks of empty pint glasses. She'd chosen this over learning about his sister, Jamal thought as he watched her pick up a dart and aim, one eye closed. She let the dart go. It bounced off the target and clattered onto the floor. She laughed loudly at her mistake. Was this what Marli did on the nights she wasn't with him? The guy aimed his dart and it hit a cluster of red feathers on the 40-point ring. "Game," he shouted, taking the last gulp from his beer glass and then pushing himself and Marli against the brick wall for a victory kiss.

"Cool it, Jackson," Marli said, pushing her classmate away with a laugh. I can take care of myself, Jamal remembered her once saying as she climbed out of his window after one of their trysts. Was this what she meant? She tugged her bra strap up and headed toward the bathroom. Jamal jumped down from his stool and followed her from a distance, waiting in front of the women's door until a line of girls started to form and one of them began to watch him suspiciously. He slipped into the men's restroom and threw some water on his face, staring at his reflection in the dirty mirror. He was drunk, not as drunk as Marli appeared to be, but not as clear-headed as he liked to be either. His roommates often told him that he misread situations, so he wasn't sure how to read this one, and what it was that he was supposed to do next.

There was no sign of Marli when he returned to the bar. Jamal made his way back to the dartboard, but even the empty glasses were gone. He plucked the winning dart from the board, staring into the black center as he ran his thumb against the tip and then dropped it into his pocket. Once Leila had been the good twin, filled with an earnest desire to please. The way she never broke rules or disappointed their parents used to drive him crazy, but now, all of the time they'd spent together—the arguments and confidences—were in question. Had his sister put herself in danger, made herself a target?

He began to imagine his sister's demise, playing out gruesome scenarios in his head: her lover a terrorist, Leila kidnapped by Shiite militia while riding a taxi to Shorjah market, or pursued by American GIs after dark, pressing her against walls, shoving her into dingy rooms. I can take care of myself, the letter seemed to suggest. Yet, images of torture—hands-bound, a black hood placed over his sister's head —bombarded him so quickly that Jamal winced.

Passing a cluttered bulletin board, he yanked at a notice for a lost German shepherd. Trigger, clenching a red ball in his jaw and worth a $250 reward, reminded Jamal of the dogs that ran in packs in certain parts of Baghdad. There, they were considered unclean and dangerous nuisances, but here dogs were family. Americans put up photographs of missing people and pets and bikes side by side on almost anything—train station walls, milk cartons, slips of paper mailed with coupons. He remembered the news coverage of 9/11, the walls of faces serving as memorials and pleas for someone to remember a stranger in the chaos. How many of those faces—those loved ones—were ever found alive? He tossed the notice down on the ground, allowing himself to wonder if it would have been better if he'd never received the letter from his sister. Women were liars. Out back, he stabbed the dart into the back tire of Marli's cruiser.

Jamal gave his sister several days and then a week and then two weeks to let him know what to do next. During that time, he missed an assignment deadline and a meeting with his advisor. He ignored his parents' calls and barely spoke to his roommates. Marli never came to his window. There was nothing to do but wait and that made the waiting that much more excruciating. Since the letter, Arabic, the language he had once loved and associated with Leila, no longer spoke to him in the same way. Now it was a taunt, a closed door he was destined to knock at forever. There was nothing for him to read. Nothing for him to write. The fall semester had begun, but he didn't care. An official-looking letter from the department sat unopened on his nightstand.

Each day, his state of mind moved closer to the time before he received his sister's letter. The worst of it was that he found himself blaming Leila for whatever had happened, the way she had allowed her life to become so full of conjecture. Because that's how it felt for

Jamal: his sister's absence had become more real and believable than the twenty-three years of her existence.

Only when his roommates had left for the evening did he come out of his room. Sitting on the batik-clad couch in a stupor, Jamal was more convinced than ever that Leila was not coming back. As he turned over her envelope for the umpteenth time, the lock of hair fell into his lap. He tried to sweep it into his hands, but it scattered. He stepped into the night, ringing with cicadas and autumn parties. As he walked, he felt for Leila's letter in his pocket. It had returned his sister to him as a stranger, only to take her away again. He wished he'd never received it. He would never mention it to his parents.

He walked down several streets of brick homes and rundown Victorian rentals, taking a turn at the food co-op, not stopping until he was on the street that Marli had described to him so carefully. It had been several weeks since he'd last seen her. She'd disappeared from his life just as his sister had. The yeast smell of baking bread and scones wafted out of the open back door of Zingerman's. When he spotted her bicycle locked to the porch rail of a house, its back tire repaired, he knew she was home. Fireflies blinked over the lawn. He climbed the stairs to the front door. He had no idea what he would say when he saw her. He was upset about what he'd seen at the bar, but more than that, hurt and confused, even worried, by her absence.

He rang the doorbell and a girl with a buzz cut opened the door and let him in. Marli's living room was very much like his—everything hand-me-down and from somewhere else, the undoubtedly stained and ripped couch draped, the mantel filled with Indian brass and Mexican silver. Chili-shaped lights were strung above the window and a large velvet curtain drawn across an archway that must have once separated the living room from the dining room. It was toward this curtain that the girl pointed when he said Marli's name.

Stepping through the drape, Jamal was surprised at the Spartan orderliness of the small room. There was a mattress on the floor covered with a white down comforter, a small drafting table with a gooseneck light clamped to the side. Her models were nowhere in sight. Instead, old books were stacked in neat piles on the floor and bed. Jamal recognized them as the emeritus books she must have been surreptitiously lugging home rather than returning to the library basement. He'd always wondered at the heaviness of her backpack. He thought of the sign over Mutanabbi Street: THIEVES DO NOT READ. Marli, the thief, was seated cross-legged on her bed in a pair of boxer shorts, slicing a square well into the pages of one of these books with an X-Acto knife.

"You can't do that," he said out of surprise.

She looked up at him without a word. For once she wasn't smiling. When he said nothing more, she returned to her work as if he wasn't there.

"You're the one who put a dart in my tire, aren't you?" she finally asked.

"You let that guy kiss you at the bar."

"I knew it," she tapped the page with the tip of the blade.

"Why would you do that?" Jamal asked.

"It felt good. The question is: Why did you just watch me? Why didn't you say anything, confront me? Aren't I worth a little trouble?"

I was jealous, he wanted to say. "Do you pick up guys like that all of the time?" he asked.

She breathed through her nose, setting the book down between them and looking squarely into his eyes. "No, sometimes they're like you."

"What do you mean by that?"

Marli began to tug at the window she'd cut into the pages, cleaning the edges. Marli, with her see-through underwear, Marli of odd hours and stolen books, Marli who didn't resist but went ahead with a kiss because it felt good. The two of them were so different. How could they ever understand each other?

"Books and buildings are not so different, you know. They're structures, ways to contain content. That's what I'm trying to say with this project." She carefully set two book covers open at 45‑degree angles so that they formed walls and then she balanced another open and face down on the top like a roof. The author of the book was none other than Dr. Sigmund Vann, the German title translated roughly as *The Last Voice in the Village*. Marli sat quietly for a moment and then shifted her weight slightly, so that they all tumbled.

"House of cards," she said.

"Tower of Babel," Jamal replied.

"You're an asshole."

"Why would you say that?"

"You think I don't pay attention, but I do. You think I'm the slut? You think that I'm using you? Be honest with yourself. Do you know what you want from me?"

"I just don't understand the rules."

"You're worried about rules? Don't you get it? We make up our own rules. Would you want some guy to treat your *sister* the way you've been treating me?"

"But, my sister would never—," he began before realizing that he did not know how to finish the sentence. He shook his head, thinking of the dart in Marli's tire. She was right. He was pretty sure he would never know what Leila would have done or what had happened to her, only that she had dared to be happy. This was the single certainty her letter offered if Jamal could only accept it. Tears filled his eyes as he sank down onto the corner of Marli's bed.

"Does this mean you're sorry?" she asked, pressing a finger into his chest.

He nodded emphatically, using her hand to stop the tears run‑ning down his cheek. He tried to imagine his sister's face, touched tenderly by the young man she loved.

"My sister," he began slowly, "She is. No, she was—." He be‑gan to cry into his hands.

"She was what?" Marli's voice was soft, yet urgent, as she tried to pry his hands open and lift his face. "Tell me. Is your sister OK?"

"In love," Jamal managed through the sobs.

Marli wrapped her arms around him. When he was calm, she dried his face with the hem of her T-shirt. He wasn't sure when he would be ready to tell her about Leila's secret, only that he would. Eventually, Marli's roommate turned off the television and pattered down the short hall to her room.

"I'm sorry," he whispered.

Marli put her hand over his mouth. "Sorry isn't good enough." She pushed him down on the bed, straddling him so that he had to look up at her. It was then that he noticed her models, tacked upside down to the ceiling above them. Mostly white, they were made of carefully creased matte boards and balsam wood with tiny trees that looked as if they were growing from the sky. The various scenes threatened to tumble down on him as if in a broken dream.

She tugged off his jacket and unbuttoned his shirt. They kissed and wrestled. Every once in a while, Marli stopped to threaten or accuse him with things like, "Never do that to me again," and "You owe me thirty-five bucks for the tire," and "I didn't deserve that," and "You're lucky to have me." Jamal agreed to it all, baffled by his pleasure and wondering if this was love. How would he know?

As Marli traced the dark hairs up his forearms and across his chest to his nipples, Jamal gave in to the irritating chill, sliding his face down between her breasts and then lower, putting his tongue into the tidy indentation of her belly button. When Marli's hips unhinged, he slid up her torso. Around them, the books gave off their musty, inky scent. His coat with Leila's letter in the pocket was tangled at their feet. A page ripped beneath Jamal's knee, another stuck to his palm. Above them, an empty city hovered.

acknowledgments

The early readers of this book provided generous comments on the stories in this collection, especially Maria Hummel, Matthew Iribarne, Katharine Noel, Jeff O'Keefe, and Malena Watrous. Scott Hutchins and Yishai Seidman encouraged me to keep going when I believed I was done. The University of San Francisco and my colleagues in Art History/Arts Management and Museum Studies provided essential support and inspiration, especially Nell Herbert. Arabic scholar and editor Yusuf Mullick kindly provided linguistic guidance. Hamza Al-Haidari graciously helped me understand more deeply Iraqi culture, the city of Baghdad, and the way that life continues even through war. This book is here thanks to Amina Gautier, as well as Ryan Kaune, Christine Stroud, and others at Autumn House who ushered it into the world with care and intelligence. I am fueled and buoyed by the love of my parents, the ongoing conversation with my husband Michael, and the embrace of my daughter Olive, who as a toddler held her arms up in the air and named this book. To all, I am enormously grateful.

This work of fiction was imagined in the safety of my California home. I am indebted to the citizens of Iraq and the American soldiers who told their stories of the war, as well as to the filmmakers, journalists, writers, and photographers who recorded these narratives in brave, honest, and artful ways. Among the many exceptional accounts, several stand out in my mind as essential to my understanding of that world. These include the films *Iraq in Fragments* directed by James Longley, *Hell and Back Again* directed by Danfung Dennis, and *The Invisible War* directed by Kirby Dick; the books *Night Draws Near: Iraq's People in the Shadow of America's War* by Anthony Shadid, *Voices from Iraq: A People's History, 2003-2009* compiled by Mark Kukis,

Black Hearts: One Platoon's Descent into Madness in Iraq's Triangle of Death by Jim Frederick, Nine Parts of Desire: The Hidden World of Islamic Women by Geraldine Brooks, and Unembedded: Four Independent Photojournalists on the War in Iraq by Ghaith Abdul-Ahad, Kael Alford, Thorne Anderson, and Rita Leistner; and, finally, the exhibition Eye Level in Iraq: Photographs by Kael Alford and Thorne Anderson. Along the way, there were many, many more.

The following stories were first published in earlier versions:
"Female Driver," The Cincinnati Review
"Night Vision," The Masters Review
"Peaches," Stumbling and Raging: More Politically Inspired Fiction, MacAdam/Cage

Fawzi Karim's "The Scent of Berries," translated by Rebecca Johnson, was excerpted from the September 2005 issue of the online journal Words without Borders.

2017 & 2018 releases

Apocalypse Mix by Jane Satterfield
  *Winner of the 2016 Autumn House Poetry Prize,
  selected by David St. John

Heavy Metal by Andrew Bourelle
  *Winner of the 2016 Autumn House Fiction Prize,
  selected by William Lychack

RUN SCREAM UNBURY SAVE by Katherine McCord
  *Winner of the 2016 Autumn House Nonfiction Prize,
  selected by Michael Martone

The Moon is Almost Full by Chana Bloch

Vixen by Cherene Sherrard

The Drowning Boy's Guide to Water by Cameron Barnett
  *Winner of the 2017 Rising Writer Prize,
  selected by Ada Limón

The Small Door of Your Death by Sheryl St. Germain

Darling Nova by Melissa Cundieff
  *Winner of the 2017 Autumn House Poetry Prize,
  selected by Alberto Ríos

Carry You by Glori Simmons
  *Winner of the 2017 Autumn House Fiction Prize,
  selected by Amina Gautier

Paper Sons by Dickson Lam
  *Winner of the 2017 Autumn House Nonfiction Prize,
  selected by Alison Hawthorne Deming

For our full catalog please visit: http://www.autumnhouse.org

design and production

Text and cover design: Chiquita Babb

Cover art: "Hand of Fatima II" courtesy of Ayad Alkadhi.
www.aalkadhi.com

Author photograph: Michael Kinomoto

The interior text of this book was typeset in Deepdene; the cover display and text was typeset in Futura. Deepdene, an oldstyle serif font, was designed by Frederic Goudy between 1927 and 1934. Futura, a geometric sans serif typeface released in 1927, was designed by Paul Renner as a contribution on The New Frankfurt, a housing settlement project that today is internationally respected as an example of early modernism in Germany.

This book was printed by McNaughton & Gunn on 55 lb. Glatfelter Natural.